"I wish you

Wyatt's steps f
his lungs. He swore his heart squeezed tight. *Me, too, bud. Me, too.*

Then he wondered if Frankie had heard what Johnny said. How would she feel about that?

Frankie led the way to her suite, then opened the door. Wyatt followed her to Johnny's room, and helped her get him settled for bed.

All tucked in bed, Johnny suddenly grabbed Wyatt's hand. "Don't leave."

"You need to get some sleep, bud."

"Just a little while? Please, Mommy? Can't you both stay?"

Frankie looked at him, a question in her eyes.

"Sure."

Frankie took off her shoes and laid down next to Johnny, gathered him in her arms. Wyatt pried his boots off, then lay behind her, and pulled them both close.

Is this what he wanted? A family? To be responsible for not just a wife, but a child...

Dear Reader,

Welcome back to the Sullivan Guest Ranch in Montana! This is the second book in my Cowboys to Grooms series with Harlequin Western Romance about brothers Nash, Kade, Wyatt, Luke and Hunter. Nash's story was my first in the series—*A Family for the Rancher.*

This is Wyatt's story—he's my rebel cowboy. He left home at seventeen, an angry young man with a learning disability, roaring out of the ranch on a motorcycle. He's back in Montana now after realizing this is where he needs to be, mending physical and familial fences with his dad and four brothers, and trying to put his past behind him.

Francine Wentworth is a top executive at her father's company in New York. They are working on a big merger and want absolute secrecy, so they've come to the ranch for business meetings. Francine has brought her adorable four-year-old son, John Allen—I adore this kid! She's torn between her job and having time with her son, but Wyatt shows her how to relax and have fun with both of them. And she even learns how to wrangle cows, too!

I hope you all enjoy returning to the Sullivans in Montana, and that you fall a little bit in love with Wyatt—as much as I did.

Happy reading!

Allison

FALLING FOR THE REBEL COWBOY

———

ALLISON B. COLLINS

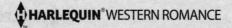

HARLEQUIN® WESTERN ROMANCE

Recycling programs
for this product may
not exist in your area.

ISBN-13: 978-1-335-69973-2

Falling for the Rebel Cowboy

Copyright © 2018 by Allison B. Collins

All rights reserved. Except for use in any review, the reproduction or utilization of this work in whole or in part in any form by any electronic, mechanical or other means, now known or hereafter invented, including xerography, photocopying and recording, or in any information storage or retrieval system, is forbidden without the written permission of the publisher, Harlequin Enterprises Limited, 22 Adelaide St. West, 40th Floor, Toronto, ON M5H 4E3, Canada.

This is a work of fiction. Names, characters, places and incidents are either the product of the author's imagination or are used fictitiously, and any resemblance to actual persons, living or dead, business establishments, events or locales is entirely coincidental.

This edition published by arrangement with Harlequin Books S.A.

For questions and comments about the quality of this book, please contact us at CustomerService@Harlequin.com.

® and TM are trademarks of Harlequin Enterprises Limited or its corporate affiliates. Trademarks indicated with ® are registered in the United States Patent and Trademark Office, the Canadian Intellectual Property Office and in other countries.

Printed in U.S.A.

Allison B. Collins is an award-winning author and a fifth-generation Texan, so it's natural for her to love all things Western. It's a tough job to spend evenings writing about cowboys, rodeos and precocious children, but Allison is willing to do it to bring them all to life. She lives in Dallas with her hero husband of almost thirty years, who takes great care of her and their four rambunctious cats.

Books by Allison B. Collins

Harlequin Western Romance

Cowboys to Grooms

A Family for the Rancher

Visit the Author Profile page
at Harlequin.com for more titles.

Acknowledgments

The old saying "It takes a village" is absolutely true,
even for writers who lead a solitary life,
entrenched in the lives of their characters.

First and foremost, I couldn't have written this book
without my amazing friends and critique partners
Suzanne Clark, Angela Hicks and Sasha Summers.
Thank you for the countless hours of brainstorming,
critiquing, texting, emailing, and for always
being there. I love you, ladies!

Thank you to my wonderful editor,
Johanna Raisanen, for believing
in me and my cowboy heroes.
It's such a pleasure working with you!

I reached out to my Facebook friends to help name
Wyatt's horse. I loved the suggestion of "Deacon"
given by Dan Hill. Thanks, Uncle Dan! Deacon is
exactly what Wyatt would have named his horse.

As always, thank you to my husband for
being my rock. You are the love of my life.

And to my readers, thank you for being
a part of my journey as an author!

Dedication

This book is dedicated to Angela Ackerman and
Rebecca Puglisi, for giving authors everywhere—
especially me!—the game-changing resources to
delve deep into our characters and make them
memorable. You know I'm your #1 fan!

Chapter One

Wyatt Sullivan stared at the beauty on the grass, glistening in the Montana sun. He knew each part of her intimately—he'd had his hands on every inch of her more times than he could count. With some pampering and TLC, he would get her purring beneath him again. After all, they didn't make tractors like this nowadays.

The sound of metal hitting metal clanged behind him, echoing like iron bars slamming shut at lights-out. The old fear roared back and his hands fisted, ready to defend. Chills sharp as barbed wire gripped his neck and galloped down his spine. He tilted his head up to the sky and blew out a calming breath, reminding himself he was safe, back home again.

He'd been a headstrong seventeen-year-old when he'd left, chucked it all, headed out on his own. But after ten years he was back, trying to find his place on the ranch with his dad and four brothers. It had taken him a long time to figure out that this ranch was home. Despite the struggles to fit back in, this was where he belonged.

Click click click echoed on the concrete path from the lodge. A woman crossed into his line of sight, her voice floating to him on a gust of wind. He'd always had a thing for blondes, and this one was real pretty. A pale pink jacket molded itself to her sleek body, and a matching skirt ended midthigh, revealing legs he could explore for days. Then her sharp words became clear.

"I was a fool to have married you. I should have listened to my father from the beginning. But we're divorced, and I'm stronger and smarter now. I won't let you treat our son like he doesn't matter."

The path curved, but she must have been distracted with her phone call, because she stepped off the concrete, still giving her ex a tongue-lashing. She was heading for the dirt of the soon-to-be vegetable garden. The one currently filled with mud from the heavy rain last night.

He followed, trailing after not only her voice, but some type of spicy perfume. He kind of liked it, and he imagined what it would smell like up close on her skin. Like behind her ear, or at the curve of her breast.

He had to grin as she tried to walk across the grass, her fancy pink heels sinking down with every step. Definitely more suited to a runway than a cattle ranch. She stumbled and lurched like a newborn foal trying to gain its legs.

"Ma'am, you might want—"

She flung a hand up at him and continued berating her ex on the phone.

"Watch out!" he called.

She turned around, glanced up at him and stepped back, mid-tirade. The icepick heel on her fancy pink shoe snapped. Teetering back, her arms wind-milled faster and faster and faster.

He sprinted toward her, even though a little mud might take this princess down a notch.

Or ten.

He grabbed for her hand but missed, snatching nothing more than air.

Gravity kept sucking her down, down, down, and she kept going, slow motion, as she lost the battle.

"Dammit, dammit, dammit," she screamed.

She landed on her back, spread-eagle, in the ooey-gooey mud.

Her cell phone plopped in front of him. He picked it up and heard a man's voice still yelling. "She'll get back to you later," he said, then ended the call.

She glared, her pretty blue eyes narrowed at him. It wouldn't have surprised him if the ground beneath her started bubbling and boiling like a big pot of stew.

He smothered a laugh, saying, "Hope you enjoy your mud bath, compliments of Sullivan Guest Ranch. Ma'am."

COLD SLUDGE OOZED and squished beneath Francine Wentworth every time she moved. *Can this day get any worse?*

A snort broke the silence, and she frowned up at the cowboy standing above her, but he just stared at her—tall, dark and brooding. The epitome of James Dean's rebel, he silently held out a hand to her.

She tried to sit up, but the mud held tight, and she felt like a pig wallowing around in muck. A lock of hair blew into her face and stuck. She tried to huff it away, but it wouldn't budge. Wrenching one arm free, she scraped the strand off her face.

She heard a strangled grunt and glanced up at the cowboy. He coughed and rubbed a hand over his mouth. But another strangled sound erupted from him, and he snapped his mouth shut, cleared his throat. *Seriously? This guy better not start laughing at me.*

Not two seconds later, said guy lost the battle and did start laughing—a deep rumbling laughter that did funny things to her insides. Even though she threw him her best *I'm going to kill you* glare, it made him hoot even harder until he was gasping for breath.

The guy kept right on at it, and every time she'd think he was done, he'd look at her and start whooping it up again.

"Are you going to help me up or just stand there like an idiot?" she asked, finally pushing herself to a sitting position. The slimy filth slid down the back of her neck, beneath the collar of her blouse, all the way down her spine, making her skin prickle. She reached back and felt her hair hanging in clumpy mats.

Her throat tightened. She hated it when she hit the boiling point, so angry that all she could do was cry. And it didn't help that this guy was still standing over her, guffawing at her mud-covered misery.

She clenched her fists tight, the wet dirt oozing through her fingers, and without thinking she flung two globs of the stuff straight at him. The mud missed his face and landed on his already-stained white T-shirt. Which only set him off into another round of that rumbling laughter.

That's it! Scooping up another fistful from the ground, she lobbed it at him. This time her aim was true, and it landed on his cheek.

"Ma'am." He wiped his hand across his face, smearing it even more. "I'm real sorry, you just—you got a little something on your face." He gestured to his upper lip.

Great. A mud mustache? She swiped the back of her wrist across her face but knew she'd just made it worse. If this set off another fit from him, she might scream.

"Are you done yet?" she asked.

He wiped his eyes. "Sorry." He held a dirt-covered hand out to her…a hand with long, strong fingers that could *definitely* make her scream—in a good way.

Wait, what?

Mesmerized, she stared at his hand until he withdrew it. He grabbed a rag from his back pocket and made a show of wiping his hands.

He held up somewhat cleaner fingers. "There. Better?"

"Never mind. I can get up all by myself."

She drew her legs up to stand, but her shoes skated over the surface of the mud pit and squelched. She glanced at her beautiful brand-new pink Dior suit. Ruined. She'd loved this suit. It had made her feel feminine and business-like all at once. Now it was destined for the trash heap.

"Might be easier if you take off your shoes."

Her spirits sank even further. Her once pristine shell-pink Blahniks, barely out of the box, were hopelessly ruined, as well. She reached down and removed each one.

Once they were off, she couldn't help it and cradled them to her chest. "Bye-bye, babies," she whispered.

"If you want, we can give them a proper burial in the family cemetery later. There might be some old boots buried out there to keep your girlie shoes company."

This guy was still making fun of her? After that call from her ex, she wasn't in the mood. She opened her mouth to tear him a new one—having grown up with a father who excelled in the subject, she knew she could do it right.

But the lazy grin on his full lips made her rusty girl parts sit up and take notice—she'd bet anything he knew how to use those lips to a woman's advantage. Involuntarily, her toes curled, squishing in the mud beneath her.

His gaze shifted to her feet. At least she'd taken the time to get a pedicure before her flight to Nowheresville, Montana.

He continued staring at her hot pink–tipped toes before his eyes drifted slowly up her legs, and she calculated just how long it'd been since a man—any man—had seen her horizontal.

Too long.

Way too long.

His slow perusal continued, and because she wanted

to spread her thighs wider, she squeezed them closer together. Her gaze was drawn laser quick to his lips curving up into a sexy, bad-boy, devil-may-care grin.

"You 'bout ready to get up outta there?"

She held her hands out, and Mr. Sexy Bad Boy's callused fingers slid over her hands and gripped as he pulled her up and out of the mud pit.

Traitorous tingles hippity-hopped up and down her spine.

"Couldn't you have warned me about that mud?" she asked, stuffing down the scary-sexy feelings about this hot-as-lava man.

"Uh, I tried, ma'am. You were kinda busy yelling on the phone."

"Don't *ma'am* me." She adjusted her jacket. "The name's Francine Wentworth. And you are?"

"Wyatt—"

Little-boy giggles reached her, and she looked down as her son ran to her side. "John Allen! What are you doing here? Why aren't you in day care?" She grabbed his hand before he fell into the pit of mud.

"Mommy! Can I play in the mud, too?" her son asked, reaching for a glob.

She huffed. "Don't do that. I had an accident."

John Allen's face crumpled, and she regretted snapping at him. Her anger drained away, leaving just embarrassment that her muddy humiliation had been witnessed by this ranch hand.

"How about we get you hosed off, Frankie?" Wyatt's voice rumbled deep as a canyon.

"My name is Francine, not Frankie," she said, with some uncontained haughtiness for good measure.

The man pushed the brim of his black cowboy hat up off his forehead, looked down at her son. "Well, seeing how she's covered head to toe in mud, I think she looks more like a Frankie right now. Whaddaya think, kid?"

John Allen looked up at her and laughed. "Yeah, mister!"

"Name's Wyatt. What's yours?" he asked, squatting down in front of her son, his jeans pulling tight on his muscled thighs.

"John Allen Wentworth," her son said, holding his hand out.

Wyatt grinned, and shook his hand. "Nice to meet you, Johnny."

What was it with this guy and nicknames?

John Allen grinned, seemingly delighted he had a nickname of his own.

WYATT UNWOUND THE hose and turned it on, letting the water flow. "Ready?"

The woman grimaced but stepped toward him without a word. He let the water run over her legs, but some of the mud had already dried and wasn't washing off. Squatting down, he ran his hand over one leg, then the next, rubbing it off. He took his time, making sure to clean off every streak of dirt.

Was it for her sake?

Or his?

"I th-think you've got it all now," she said.

Too bad. He wouldn't mind washing a few other parts of her body. He stood up and glanced at her cherry-red cheeks. "Cold?"

"A little," she said, not looking at him, and rinsed her muddy hands off under the hose.

"Francine, what is going on out here?" a man shouted behind him.

Wyatt turned to see a man in a perfectly pressed gray suit storming down the path from the lodge.

"Dammit," she whispered next to Wyatt.

Instinct had him stepping in between her and the big, angry man.

"Dad, I can explain," she said, stepping around Wyatt.

"Are you all right? Why are you all muddy?" Frankie's father whirled to face Wyatt. "What did you do to her?"

"It's nothing—" Frankie started to say.

"What's your name? I'm going to report you to the owner." Mr. Suit pulled a phone out of his pocket.

"Dad, I just tripped in the mud, and this nice man—"

"Wyatt Sullivan," he said, holding a hand out to her father, knowing damn good and well he wouldn't take it. "Part owner of Sullivan Guest Ranch."

Father and daughter glanced at him. "You are?" they asked at the same time.

He tipped his cowboy hat at her. "Yep."

"Anyway, Mr. Sullivan was helping me so I wouldn't track mud all over the lodge."

"Thank you for helping my daughter." The older man looked calmer but still had a suspicious look on his face. "You don't look like a luxury-ranch owner. Besides, I met the owner, Angus," her father said.

"That's my dad." This man didn't need to know Wyatt's share wasn't final yet. He would get it when he could prove to his dad he was home to stay.

Wentworth ignored him. "Francine, why don't you get cleaned up. We need you back in the meeting."

He looked down at his grandson. "And make sure John Allen doesn't get dirty, too." He dialed a number on his cell phone and went back the way he'd come.

"I'm really sorry, Mr. Sullivan," she said.

"Wyatt," he said, trying to keep his cool as long-forgotten rage bubbled up from his past.

"Wyatt, I apologize for my father. He can be a bit…" She bit her lip.

"Bossy?"

"He *is* my boss."

"Sorry," he said. "So, here for work, not vacation?"

"Well, it's a working retreat for us. Since we'll be here a couple of weeks, we decided to let everyone bring their families. We try to keep everyone happy."

"Where are y'all from?"

"New York City."

He blinked. "Long way to come for meetings."

"We have our reasons. Besides…" She gestured at the scenery. "It's nice to see mountains instead of skyscrapers for a change." She lifted her wrist and checked her watch. At least that wasn't ruined. "I need to get cleaned up and back to the conference room. Thanks for your help."

"You need any help getting back?"

"I think we're fine. Thank you." She took hold of her son's hand. "Come on, sweetie."

"See ya round, Johnny."

The kid beamed, his grin a mile wide. "See ya!"

Wyatt shook his head. At least the kid wasn't like Frankie's old man. Yet.

"See ya, Frankie," he called and snickered when she froze, her back going even more rigid than it had been. What was it about this woman that made him want to razz her? Was it that she seemed to take herself just a bit too seriously? He wanted to make her smile. Johnny said something to her as the two continued up the path, and she laughed, then they disappeared through the front door of the lodge.

He looked around at the buildings glowing in the late-afternoon sun. His dad and Kade had expanded the lodge while he'd been away, and the main building was at least five times bigger now. Even not knowing anything about architecture, he could tell Kade had designed it specifically for rich people. Like Ms. Francine Wentworth and her bossy father.

It wasn't exactly home anymore, with all the new guest cabins, outbuildings and bigger barns, but at least each structure was designed to blend in with the natural beauty of Montana. But he still missed the old days when it had been a small dude ranch and they had regular people come out for vacation, to learn the old ways of ranching.

Yeah, they still did cattle ranching now, and trail rides, chuck wagon dinners out in the meadows, but now instead of just families, big groups would come out for working retreats. Kade and Pop had been talking about adding spa services. This was Montana. People should come here to enjoy the land, the wildlife, the wide-open spaces.

Not for fancy treatments and crap.

Which made him think of Frankie and her hot-pink-polished toes and those long legs, a forbidden temptation.

No sense thinking about her. She'd drop him faster than a bronc busts a greenhorn once she found out about his past.

Chapter Two

Wyatt strode to the equipment barn, heels pounding like a hammer setting stakes in the ground. His dog trotted next to him and woofed. He slowed down so Sadie wasn't exerting herself in her pregnant condition.

It was a pretty day, with the sun shining, birds singing, a crisp autumn breeze lifting the hair off his neck. Yet he was too pissed to enjoy it. His lesson that morning hadn't gone well. He was finally doing something about getting his diploma, but how could he succeed when he had trouble comprehending what his tutor was teaching him?

He felt stupid.

He hated feeling stupid.

Damn learning problems.

And after that, the long email his dad had sent listing chores, talking about Wyatt's place on the ranch, had made him so mad the letters got all jumbled up when he'd tried to read it. He knew he had to wait till he calmed down to revisit it.

He huffed out a breath. After nine months of hard work, his dad still didn't trust him. He'd never get the foreman job he was hoping for.

Maybe if he was more like Kade. His second-oldest brother got along with their dad best—he was ranch manager and damn good at it. Luke, a year younger than Wyatt, did his part as the ranch veterinarian. Then there was Hunter, his youngest brother. Charmer, jokester and the glue that held everyone together. He'd missed them all while he was gone, was still trying to find his place now that he was back. He'd hoped the foreman job opening up would be it. He genuinely wanted it, and it'd prove to his family he was here to stay.

But his dad wasn't giving him a fair chance—he looked at Wyatt and saw a screwup. Acting out as a teen was one thing, but Wyatt hated thinking about his time in Texas. What had happened down there had been out of his control—his family knew it—but it didn't erase the mark that dark period had left on him, or the way his dad looked at him now. "Why'd I bother to come back here?" he muttered.

"'Cause it's your home," Nash said.

Wyatt glanced around at his oldest brother, ready to let loose with a blast of cusswords, but saw Nash's six-year-old stepdaughter, Maddy, standing next to him. She beamed at him and threw her arms up for a hug. "Good mornin', Uncle Wyatt."

Wyatt picked her up, and she smacked his cheek with a kiss. "Morning, sunshine," he said and ruffled her long dark curls. "How you doin'?" He'd never been one for kids, but he'd grown to love this little girl who shared her heart with everyone.

"Good," she said, throwing her arms around his neck and giving him her one-of-a-kind hug. He had to admit it was nice having a niece to spoil along with his four nephews.

"Where's Kelsey?"

"I got her to go back to bed. Morning sickness hit hard today," Nash said.

"Does she need a doctor?"

"She says it's normal," Nash said, but damn if his voice didn't waver a bit, and he looked a little queasy himself.

His brother had been injured and angry at the world when he got home from Afghanistan. Kelsey was the best thing that could have happened to him, and he'd fallen hard and fast for her. Now they ran a therapy program for veterans, and Nash was responsible for the horses on the ranch.

"So what's wrong?" Nash asked.

"For some reason, Pop doesn't think I know what needs to be done around here. He keeps sending emails and texts for chores that I'm already working on or planning to do. It's like I didn't grow up on a ranch with the rest of you." He handed Maddy to Nash.

"Need some help?"

"Nah. I'll just keep plugging away at it," he said, his lip curling. "Well, see y'all later. Need to get to work." Wyatt yanked open the sliding door of the equipment barn, and metal screeched. One more thing to tack on to his growing to-do list.

He slapped the wall and ran his hand up the row of switches, turning the lights on and banishing the shadows cast by the ancient tractor. The smell of oil and gasoline mixed with sawdust and wood permeated the air. It was familiar, comforting to him in many ways. Each barn had its own smell depending on what it was used for. And he loved them all.

He shucked his denim jacket and hung it on a peg by the door, then strapped on his tool belt. As he crossed the floor to the tractor, the tools clinked and jangled with every step, creating a beat in his head. He cocked his head, listening as he walked, already committing it to memory until he could get his hands on his guitar.

Sadie walked to the side of the barn where he'd set up a bed for her. She stepped onto the pad, turned around three times, then plopped down, sighing as if she'd just run a marathon with a pack of wolves. He watched her for a few minutes, made sure she was okay. He'd found her wandering one of the meadows a while back, and when no one claimed her, decided to keep her. She made a great roommate, but now their little family would be growing when she gave birth.

He turned his attention to the first item on the list. Another tractor with a problem. This one was older than the one he'd fixed the day before. He started taking the tractor's engine apart, piece by prehistoric piece, convinced there were still more years left in her. He refused to let anyone haul it off to the junkyard. One of the bolts proved stubborn, and he grabbed his hammer and banged on it, letting loose a stream of profanities.

"Hey, mister! What's that mean?"

The kid's voice startled him, and he pounded his thumb instead of the bolt. He jerked around, sticking the tenderized thumb in his mouth, and saw Frankie's kid.

"Hey, Johnny," he mumbled around his stinging thumb.

"You okay, mister? I didn't mean it," Johnny said, hanging his head.

"Not your fault, kid. My fault for getting mad at the da—dang-blasted tractor."

His thumb finally stopped throbbing, and he stuck the hammer back in his tool belt, then looked around for Frankie. "Is your mom with you?"

Johnny shook his head. "She's working."

Great, a kid wandering around a big ranch alone? Not good. "Isn't someone watching you?"

"No, sir. I was at day care. I'm bored. Can I help?"

Wyatt shook his head, knowing the child-care worker at the lodge would be frantic trying to find him. The kid was a hoot—four years old, he guessed, going on forty, with proper grammar, pressed clothes and everything. Wyatt's mom would have called the kid an old soul.

Which was a shame.

"How about I take you back up there? You don't want to miss out on any fun, do you?"

The kid looked up at him, his eyes a piercing blue. "I want to stay here." He scuffed his shoe—a loafer, for Pete's sake—at something invisible on the barn floor.

Wyatt bit the inside of his cheek, trying not to laugh even as he felt sorry for the kid. Way too young to already be like a little old man.

Sadie woofed, and Johnny looked at her. "You got a dog?" he asked, already racing over to her side. He stopped short, then reached a little hand out for her to sniff. Sadie looked up at the boy, and Wyatt could have sworn she smiled.

"Mister, can I pet her?"

"Sure. Her name's Sadie."

Johnny crouched down next to her and patted her head. "I love dogs."

"You and your mom have a dog?"

Johnny shook his head, his chin wobbling. "No. We can't have one."

Poor kid. "Come on, let's get you back to the lodge before they call out the big guns." He walked to the door and waited while Johnny said goodbye to Sadie.

The boy patted Sadie one last time and walked to the door, dragging his feet and looking as if Santa *and* the Easter Bunny had just crossed him off their nice lists.

Wyatt squashed the guilty feelings down deep. Sure, he had nephews and a niece, but what did he really know about kids? The boys had been born while he'd been gone, so he was still trying to get to know them.

But a guest's kid? Not his pint of beer.

They reached the lodge and Wyatt took him inside to

the day care, made sure Mrs. Dailey had him in hand, then retraced his path to the barn.

As he walked inside, he checked on Sadie, and damned if she didn't look like she was frowning at him.

Grabbing the wrench off the seat, he went back to working on the tractor in peace. He settled back in to work, losing himself in the task of stripping the engine bare to find the source of the problem.

Sometime later he surfaced as a scuff quietly echoed, the noise sending goose bumps prickling along his back. The sound transported him back to a time when he'd been helpless, no defense other than his fists against men bigger than him.

He gripped the wrench tighter and casually reached for the hammer with his free hand. No one would ever take him by surprise again.

He jerked around, weapons raised, scanning for the intruder. His eyes searched the shadows until Sadie gave a soft woof, and he moved enough to see her and Johnny staring at him. How had the kid made it all the way inside the barn making so little sound?

"What are you doing back here?"

"I dunno," Johnny said, his arms going around Sadie's neck.

"You can't keep running off like that, kid. Mrs. Dailey will get upset, and your mom...well, let's just say I don't want to see her bad side."

"Huh?"

"Never mind," Wyatt said, setting the tools down on the wheel of the tractor and pulling his phone out of his pocket. He dialed the day care lady and asked for Frankie's—Francine's, he corrected—phone number.

Entering the number on his phone, he texted her to

say Johnny was down at the barn, and wouldn't stay in day care.

A few minutes later, he received a text that she'd be right there. Not more than five minutes later, she came running into the barn, once again wearing fancy shoes. On a ranch.

"John Allen Wentworth. Why did you leave the day care?"

"I don't like it there."

"Are the other kids mean to you?" He hadn't thought about that being the cause of Johnny not wanting to stay put.

The kid shook his head. "I want to stay here. With Sadie." He buried his face in the dog's shoulder.

Francine turned to Wyatt. "I don't understand why he's doing this. I'm sorry."

Wyatt studied Johnny. "Maybe he just doesn't like people? I can take 'em or leave 'em sometimes myself."

She stepped closer to him. "He's really shy. But he's never disobeyed me like this before. I don't know what to do. I'm sorry he's getting in your way."

"You okay if he stays here with me?" His words surprised himself. Surprised Miss New York as well, if the look on her face was right.

"I don't want to burden you."

He thought about it. "I'm just working on the tractor today." The kid needed to have some fun, and if he was going to keep wandering around, at least Johnny could hang around the barn so Wyatt could keep an eye on him.

She hesitated.

"Look, I know you don't know me—"

She shook her head. "That's not it. If you're sure you don't mind. I'll be down to pick him up as soon as the meeting is over later today. You've got my phone number, right?"

He nodded.

"I really appreciate it." She looked at her watch. "I need to get back. John Allen, you can stay here, but you mind Mr. Sullivan, okay? You do what he says and don't go anywhere, you hear me?" She kissed the top of her son's head.

The kid bounced up and down. "I'll be good. Promise!" He raced back to Sadie and sat down next to her.

"Thank you, Mr. Sullivan. I appreciate it."

"Wyatt."

Her nose crinkled. "What?"

"I'm Wyatt, Miz Wentworth."

"Oh, yes. Call me Francine. Thanks again. I'll see you later."

Wyatt watched her hurry up the path to the lodge until she disappeared through the doors. Must be hard for her to raise a child on her own and have to work. Kade had been doing it, but at least they lived here at the ranch, with plenty of family around to help out when he needed it.

He got back to work on the tractor but checked on Johnny every few minutes.

"Mister, how come you're taking that apart?"

Johnny's words startled him, and he looked down at the kid staring up at him. "It stopped working."

"You know how to fix stuff?"

Wyatt nodded. He might not be good with reading, but he'd always had a knack for anything mechanical.

"Will you teach me?"

"Why?"

"Why not?" Johnny shrugged.

"You got any old clothes you can change into?"

Johnny shook his head.

"Any play clothes that can get dirty, and your mom won't care?"

"Play clothes?"

What was with Francine, that the kid didn't have something to play in, to be a little boy in? Her suit yesterday probably cost more than three months' pay, but her boy didn't have jeans and a T-shirt? Surely he didn't wear pressed clothes and dress shoes every day?

"How old are you?"

Johnny held up four fingers.

Wyatt pulled his phone out again and called Kade. "You still have any of Toby's old clothes from when he was about four?"

"Yeah, I think so. Why?"

"Got someone here who needs to borrow them."

"No problem. They're in the spare room at my place. Help yourself."

Wyatt pressed the end call button. "Okay, kid. Let's go. I think we can find something for you to wear."

Kade's cabin was closest to the lodge and outbuildings, and it wasn't too cold out, so Wyatt bundled Johnny into his own denim jacket and rolled the sleeves up, then they set off walking the short distance.

He let them into the cabin, and they headed upstairs to the spare room. Although, when he opened the door to the room, he changed that to *junk* room. A stack of canvases lined one wall, and the boxes Kade had mentioned were stacked on two more walls, each one neatly marked. He looked closer and saw the year had been added to each one, along with a list of the contents. Following the system his anal-retentive brother used, it was easy to find the box with Toby's clothes from when he was four.

He pulled the box down and opened it, then dug through it to find several white T-shirts, pint-size Western shirts and miniature denim jeans and jackets. Holding the jeans up to Johnny, he figured they'd fit, even if the cuffs had to be rolled up some. Digging into the box farther, he found small cowboy boots and socks. Another box yielded several old cowboy hats.

"What do you think? Wanna wear a hat, too?"

Johnny's eyes lit up, rivaling Fourth of July sparklers. "Really? Yeah! Thanks, mister!"

"Call me Wyatt," he said, feeling old, even though he was only in his late twenties.

Johnny beamed. "Thanks, Mr. Wyatt!"

"Let's get you changed and get back to work, okay?"

The kid grinned and unbuttoned his blue shirt, then pulled on the T-shirt and a brown Western shirt.

"So do you go to school yet?"

Johnny nodded.

"Let me guess. You're in college, right? Graduating soon?"

Johnny giggled. "No, sir. I go to preschool." He grinned, and Wyatt noticed a gap where he'd lost a tooth.

"What do you do for fun?"

The kid cocked his head. "Um, piano lessons."

"Do you like it?"

He shook his head. "No."

"How come?"

"My teacher's really old and smells like paper."

Wyatt grinned. "I must have had the same teacher as you. Or maybe they were sisters. She'd be about a hundred and fifty now."

Johnny nodded, his face solemn. "That's how old Mrs. Jenkins is, too."

Wyatt laughed, and Johnny looked surprised. He sat the little boy down on the chair and rolled the denim cuffs up, then helped him put on the boots.

He held up three miniature cowboy hats. "Which do you want to wear?"

Johnny looked at all three, then up at Wyatt's own hat, and pointed at the black one.

He set it on Johnny's head, then tapped the brim. "Fit good?"

"Yes, sir."

"Then let's get back to work, bud."

Wyatt led the way back out, then locked up. As they walked back to the main area, he noticed his long strides were making Johnny trot to keep up. He reached down and lifted Johnny up onto his shoulders.

Johnny squealed and grabbed Wyatt's hair.

"You okay, pal?"

"I never done this! It's fun!"

And with that, Wyatt's heart broke a little for this kid who seemed a rookie to fun.

FRANCINE GLANCED DOWN at her phone for what had to be the hundredth time, making sure Wyatt hadn't texted her. She'd been so surprised he'd said John Allen could stay with him.

She took a deep breath and blew it out slowly. Lately John Allen had been restless and hadn't wanted to stay in preschool. She suspected it was because he was so painfully shy, but she'd followed the suggestion of the teachers and had him tested. The full results weren't back yet, but everyone agreed he was very smart for his age and was most likely bored at the level he was being taught.

Looking up, she caught her father staring at her, concerned. She shook her head and smiled. She'd have to have a long talk with John Allen tonight about wandering off.

She forced her attention back to the report in front of her. This merger was really important to the future of Wentworth & Associates. It would give them a stronger team and make them one of the most influential investment groups in the country.

But things weren't going well, and they'd already discovered one corporate spy a few weeks ago. So they'd packed everyone up and come to Montana for a working vacation, away from any underhandedness in New York. The team they'd brought here were all trusted associates, on both sides of the negotiating table. And to keep them happy about working out of state so close to the holidays— without weekends, so they could stay on track—their families had been invited.

It had been a shock when her dad's assistant had found a luxury ranch in the middle of nowhere with plenty of availability for the entire group. Too bad she had to keep her head in the game, or she would've enjoyed the ranch amenities more.

Harvey Knight spoke up. He was the president of Knightsbridge, the other investment group Wentworth was merging with. She studied him, his body language. The man was older than her father; even though he looked healthy, he had an air of fragility around him. He'd told her dad he was ready to retire, enjoy his grandchildren and wife after working too many years under too much pressure. He'd guaranteed that he'd announce his retirement once the merger was complete, as long as all of his associates remained with the company. This retreat was also a way of making sure everyone got along.

She turned her attention to the rest of the team. Today was a smaller meeting with the top executives in both companies, so only eight surrounded the conference table. A few power clashes had sprung up, and it was her job to evaluate how everyone would mesh. The benefits of a minor in psychology had granted her that unenviable position.

Her counterpart, Peter Yates, the executive vice president of Knightsbridge, definitely had a temper. How he'd fit in with the rest of her team, she wasn't sure at this point. He'd brought his wife and teenage daughter, who definitely looked like a handful, with him to Montana.

Then again, she was looking at two weeks with a wandering son, an impending merger and her father's mood swings to deal with—a handful of her own.

Three exhausting hours later, they finally decided to call it a day. She stacked her notes together and put them in a leather portfolio, then stood up and headed out to pick up John Allen.

Her heels clicked on the concrete sidewalk as she walked toward the barns, and she caught a ranch hand smirking at her outfit. She remembered Wyatt commenting on her shoes yesterday. What did they expect? She was a VP here for work, and she needed to look the part. Besides, she loved her designer wardrobe.

As she neared the big red equipment barn, she stopped at the most unlikely thing she'd ever seen. The barn doors were wide-open, and Wyatt Sullivan stood in front of a red tractor that had to be a hundred years old. His back was to her, his hands on his hips, booted feet spread apart, looking as if he was scrutinizing the tractor. *He definitely fills out a pair of jeans.*

But it was the pint-size boy standing next to him that had her biting her tongue. Dressed exactly like Wyatt, her son wore old jeans, a brown Western shirt, tiny boots and a smaller version of Wyatt's black cowboy hat. His posture mirrored Wyatt's.

Even as she watched, John Allen turned his head and looked up at Wyatt, just as Wyatt used a finger to tip the brim of his hat up so it rested on the back of his head. Her son raised his little hand and did the exact same thing, and they both went back to staring at the tractor.

"What do ya say, bud? Shall we start her up, make sure it works?"

John Allen looked up at him, his face very serious. "Yup."

Wyatt grabbed a couple of rags off the bench next to him and handed one to her son. John Allen watched him carefully as Wyatt wiped his greasy hands on the rag, then followed his exact movements.

She slipped her phone out of her suit pocket and took photos of the pair together. The last thing she wanted was John Allen hanging around large equipment, but he looked so cute she had to capture the image.

Wyatt turned around then and saw her watching them. He tipped his cowboy hat at her. "Ma'am," he drawled.

John Allen tipped his hat at her, as well. "Mommy," he drawled. Then grinned as big as she'd ever seen him. "Mr. Wyatt fixed the trak-ter, and I helped!"

"You did? Wow. I'll bet Mr. Wyatt sure appreciated your help today." She glanced up to see Wyatt watching her. His eyes were so deep, almost fathomless pools, and she wondered what he was thinking.

"Where did those clothes come from?"

"They're my nephew's hand-me-downs—didn't want to ruin Johnny's fancy clothes."

"Fancy clothes?"

"His little *GQ Junior* outfit."

"Oh," she said, embarrassment burning her cheeks at not having thought to bring any jeans or tennis shoes for her son. He rarely wore them in New York.

"We were just about to start the tractor up and take a spin around the field. You okay with that, Francine?"

"I don't think that's a very good idea." She looked up

at how high the seat was on the tractor. "John Allen snuck away from day care twice today, and he knows better than that."

Her son's smile collapsed, and his chin wobbled. "I'm sorry, Mommy. Please? Can I go?" He looked up at her, beseeching her, with hands clasped together as if in prayer.

Wyatt shifted, and he clasped his hands together, mirroring John Allen this time. "Please, Mom? I'll be real careful with him." He stepped forward, hooking his thumbs in his belt loops. "Kid needs to have some fun, and he really did help me today."

She looked at him, frowning. How on earth could her baby help fix a tractor?

"Oh, all right. But not for long. We need to get you cleaned up for dinner."

John Allen jumped up and down, and his hat fell off. Wyatt picked it up and plunked it back on his head, then lifted him up high, onto the seat of the tractor. Wyatt climbed up and sat down, then pulled John Allen onto his lap.

"Hold on tight, sweetie. And you do exactly what Mr. Wyatt says, okay?"

Her son bounced up and down and looked so excited— as if it was his birthday, Christmas and Halloween all rolled into one day.

Wyatt started the old tractor, and it grunted and groaned, maybe even screamed a little, belching black smoke, and she quickly backed out of the way. As the tractor rolled out of the barn, Wyatt whooped, waving his hat in the air. John Allen followed suit, and she snapped a few more pictures as they continued down the drive and out into an empty field.

She continued watching them, enjoying the late-afternoon sun as it turned everything a gold hue. Her stomach growled, and she knew John Allen had to be hungry. But a few minutes more wouldn't hurt, would it?

The tractor turned and headed back to the barn, just as she thought she heard her name over the roar of the engine.

"Francine. What are you doing?" her father asked, coming up the path toward her. He started to say something else, but the engine drowned out his voice, for which she was grateful.

"Mommy! Did you see me? Did you see me?" John Allen squealed as Wyatt stopped the tractor next to them.

"What the—" her father said. "Why is my grandson on that tractor? It's dangerous."

She glanced at him, alarmed at how red his face was. His blood pressure had skyrocketed the last few years from too much work and stress.

"Get down right now, young man," her father called.

Wyatt looked from her father to her, climbed down from the behemoth, then lifted her son down. John Allen's face crumpled, and his eyes glistened with tears. He crowded up against Wyatt's legs. His move shocked her more than anything—John Allen usually preferred to play alone. He'd taken to Wyatt so quickly.

Wyatt laid a hand on his shoulder and patted it. "It's okay, bud. I'll bet your granddad was just surprised to see you riding up on this big ol' tractor. He doesn't know you were a big help to me today."

His words were calm, but his voice had a slight edge and his expression was closed off.

She set her hand on her dad's arm, felt the tension running through his tendons like thick coiled rope. He shook her off, and she stepped back.

"John Allen, you're a Wentworth, not a ranch hand. You're going to be an important part of my company someday, not a common mechanic."

"Dad!" she said, embarrassed to no end at his thoughtless words. "Wyatt—er, Mr. Sullivan and John Allen were having fun today."

Her father turned to Wyatt. "What right do you have taking my grandson out of day care? I ought to have you arrested." Even as he uttered the threat, he pulled out his cell phone.

Wyatt's hands fisted at his sides, and he took a step forward—big, tall, intimidating and very scary. He reminded her of an outlaw—and with his long dark hair and black cowboy hat, he definitely fit the image of a rebel cowboy.

She stepped between them, raising her arms to the side like a referee at an MMA match. "I gave permission for John Allen to be here."

Her father slowly put his mobile back into his pocket. "I don't want this to happen again. He's my grandson and I'm making sure he's on the right path for success." He turned to her, and it took everything she had to keep her back straight. "Francine, take him up to the lodge and get him cleaned up. I want to debrief on this last meeting before dinner." He turned on his heel and strode back up the path to the main lodge.

Dreading it, but knowing she had to get it over with, she turned to Wyatt. He'd knelt down and was consoling her son, something she should be doing. John Allen threw his arms around Wyatt's neck and squeezed. Since he was facing her, the shocked look on Wyatt's face surprised her, but it was soon followed by sweet tenderness as he hugged her baby back.

"I'm so sorry, Wyatt. He didn't mean what he said."

"Oh, I'll bet he did," Wyatt said, standing up. His face was devoid of any expression, and she never wanted to play poker with him…not that she even knew how.

"I am sorry," she said and took John Allen's hand. Words could hurt, and her father was a master at wielding them like a sword, both in the boardroom and out. "Thank you for watching him today." She took her son's hand and led him to the path that would take them to the lodge.

"My pleasure. Anytime," came the low response. When she glanced back, Wyatt was already walking away.

Chapter Three

Francine rubbed her temples, willing away the headache she'd woken up with. She glanced around the table at her coworkers, noticing the tension and stress clearly marked on everyone's faces. The merger was stalled, and at this point, for every step forward, they slid back three.

At the first lull in a heated conversation, she spoke up. "I think we all need to take a break."

Her dad glanced up, opened his mouth, then looked around the table and snapped it shut. "She's right. Take a break and come back in—" he slid his cuff up enough to see his watch "—two hours."

Sighs of relief sounded as everyone jumped up and headed for the door.

Francine stood up and stretched, grimacing at the stiffness in her back and neck. She sent a quick text to Mrs. Dailey to make sure John Allen had stayed put in day care that morning. The woman answered that he was still there, no problems. Francine breathed a sigh of relief, then crossed the room to the coffeepot, pouring yet another cup of caffeine to keep her going the rest of the day.

A movement outside the window caught her eye, and she looked out. A big truck sat in front of one of the barns, and a man stood in the back, unloading bales of hay. He'd lift a bale, then chuck it in front of the barn, where three other men hauled them inside.

Just as she took a sip of coffee, the man outside turned slightly, and she realized it was Wyatt.

Even as she watched, he grabbed a rag out of his back pocket and wiped his face, shoved it back in and grabbed up another bale of hay. His biceps flexed with each movement, and even being a city girl, she knew those bales had to weigh a lot. Yet he made it look effortless, his movements streamlined and graceful.

The weather was cool, yet he'd still sweat through his T-shirt, which now hugged his back.

It was almost hypnotic watching him, and she found herself relaxing for the first time in days.

A hand touched her shoulder and she jumped, sloshing coffee on the credenza. She grabbed several napkins and mopped it up.

"Didn't mean to scare you. I called your name three times and you never heard me. What are you looking at?" Her dad glanced out the window.

"Nothing. Just thinking about the meeting—"

He frowned. "You were watching that Sullivan boy, weren't you."

She laughed. "Dad, he's hardly a boy."

"I get it. You're a beautiful single woman, and he's a relatively—well, a decent-looking man." He rubbed a hand across the back of his neck, something he did when uncomfortable.

"Don't be ridiculous."

He looked at her, his mouth turned down in a frown. "I'm just saying, if you're going to have a—a—an encounter—"

"Dad!" Her stomach did flip-flops, and heat bloomed up her chest to explode in her cheeks.

He held a hand up to stop her words. "I don't think he's

the right type of man for you—in fact, I'm sure he's been a lot of fathers' worst nightmare."

"You don't know that, or anything about him—"

"You've been pretty quick to defend him. I'm just saying, you need to be more discreet." He became more stern, pointedly saying, "That means no ogling the ranch hands. We have a great deal riding on this merger, and I don't want any distractions or gossip."

As if she didn't know that. She was on track to be CEO one day—if anyone knew focus, it was her. And if she had imagined doing something with Wyatt—in the dark of night—the last thing she wanted was to discuss it with her father.

"I know what's at stake. I'm not planning on doing anything—"

"Good," her father said. Glancing away, he added, "I just don't want you hurt again…once is enough, trust me."

Her dad was a blunt man, but his words softened her. He'd been through a divorce when her mother left them. Over two years ago, she'd followed in his footsteps with one of her own. "Dad, I'm sorry." She slipped her arm through his and laid her head on his shoulder.

"It was a long time ago. You were too young to see it, but your mother and I were never happy together."

"We've never really talked about it. I know you've seen a few women over the years, but do you regret never marrying again?"

"No, I don't." He squeezed her hand. "Besides, even if your mother and I didn't get along, at least she gave me you. And I'm very happy about that."

She smiled. "Me, too, Dad. We make a pretty good team at Wentworth's, don't we?"

"No one I'd rather have more at my side."

"I learned from the best," she said. It was true. Her dad

could be tough, but he'd trained her from a young age to be a sharp-minded businesswoman. Oh, she'd worked hard to earn it, but she counted her blessings to be highly placed in a Fortune 500 company. It was where she and her dad connected, especially after her mother left—he'd always been there for her.

"I'll be back in a little while," her dad said. "You should go out, get some fresh air." He stopped at the door and looked back at her. "I love you, Francine. You're one hell of a businesswoman. All I ask is that you don't make a mistake you'll regret, for yourself or my grandson."

She nodded. Glancing out the window again, she noticed they had finished unloading the hay from the truck. The three men who'd been helping Wyatt stood around a cooler, drinking water and laughing at something. Wyatt was off by himself, staring out at the lake.

She and Wyatt hadn't talked much, but she could sense he usually kept to himself. John Allen had certainly taken to him quickly, and he rarely liked strangers. She'd sensed a reserve about Wyatt, much like her son's, around other people, as if he was hesitant to let himself get close to anyone.

That was probably why her son had bonded with him— and it was also a reason to stay away.

Chapter Four

Early the next morning, Francine made sure her son was at the day care, under strict orders not to leave. Her father was on a conference call to Germany when she left the lodge. She walked down the front steps, and a little pink sports car caught her attention as it sped down the road leading out of the property. *Cute car.*

Her mission of the morning was to find a way into town and buy her son some play clothes. Her dad had complained the evening before about her son wearing someone else's old worn-out clothes, even if it was just temporary. She felt a little guilty, escaping on her own, but she really needed it. Besides, it'd be fun to surprise John Allen with a cowboy hat.

"Need some help, ma'am?" Wyatt drawled from behind her.

She turned around, and he stood there, looking so much like every bad boy her father had warned her away from. Black cowboy hat, black T-shirt, denim jacket, dark hair just a bit too long, a scar slashing white on his chin—she hadn't noticed it before. His blond Labrador stood at his side staring up at her with deep brown eyes, so maybe Wyatt wasn't all bad. A country song about a man and his dog came to mind.

"As a matter of fact, I do. Does Uber come out here? I can't seem to find any drivers on the app."

His quirked eyebrow made her feel stupid.

"So...no Uber service?"

"Nope. Need a ride somewhere?" His breath puffed out in the frosty morning like cigarette smoke.

"I want to go into town and get some things for my son."

"I'm headed there. You can ride with me."

If she remembered correctly, the closest town was at least an hour away. Cooped up with him in a vehicle for that long? She pasted a smile on her face. "Thank you. That's very kind of you."

He shrugged, said, "Come on," and led the way to his black pickup truck. He opened the passenger door, then stood aside. Just as she started to climb into the truck, the blond lab jumped into the passenger seat.

"Sorry. She loves going for rides. Just give her a shove and she'll move over."

She shooed her hands at the dog, but it didn't move. "Come on, sweetie. Move over, okay?" She waved her hands again.

The dog looked at Wyatt, and he looked at the dog. If she didn't know better, she'd have sworn they both rolled their eyes. He gave a quick whistle and the dog rolled over.

Leaving a layer of blond dog hair behind on the passenger seat.

Great. Francine looked down at her black suit and Chanel coat. Wyatt reached in and moved the seat forward, and the dog jumped into the back. He brushed the seat off, then rummaged behind it, pulling out an old red plaid blanket.

"It's old but relatively free of dog hair," he said, then spread it across the seat.

"Thanks," she said and climbed up into the truck, shivering in the cold morning.

He shut the door, walked around to the driver's side and got in, then started the engine. "It'll warm up in a minute." He put the truck in gear and headed down the long drive to the main road.

"What's your dog's name?"

"Sadie."

Before long, heat poured out of the vents. "Is it always this cold?"

He lifted a shoulder. "Sometimes. It's already snowed up in the mountains."

"Do you and your family live here all year, or go elsewhere when the snow hits?"

"All year. Guests come here in winter, too."

"Doesn't it get lonely out here?"

"Nope." He turned the radio on.

She took the hint he didn't want to talk and settled back, watching the scenery roll by. Born and bred in New York City, she was used to the frenetic pace of a big urban area and millions of people. She knew concrete and crowds and skyscrapers, not mountains and valleys and lakes.

The road curved along the prairie, river and hillsides. She spotted some kind of sheep clambering up and down rocks—

Wyatt slammed on the brakes, and the truck stopped suddenly in the middle of the road. She braced a hand on the dashboard and looked out the front window.

A large herd of massive animals plodded across the road in front of them. Sadie's head appeared over the back of the seat between them, her doggy breath warm on Francine's neck. The dog yawned, ending with a squeak, then lay back down, giving a doggy sigh, as if this were a common occurrence.

"Are those buffalo?" Francine wished he'd stopped the truck about a mile back.

"Bison." Wyatt leaned back, his thumb idly tapping the beat to the song on the radio.

"They won't stampede, will they?"

"Nope."

His brief answers really irked her. Did he not believe in civilized conversation? "Gee, you're just a regular chatty Cathy. Let me guess. You do PR for the ranch, right?"

SHE WAS FEISTY. He might even appreciate it…but something told him she was used to talking down to guys like him. "That would be my brother Hunter. I don't believe in talking just to fill a silence."

She stared at him a beat, then her gaze shifted over his shoulder. Her mouth opened, and a scream ricocheted around the truck. But not just any scream. One of those *Friday the Thirteenth*–Freddy Krueger–Chucky–*Halloween* movie screams.

He whipped his head around and saw an enormous bison standing not two feet from his door, staring at them.

He held very still but slid a hand to Frankie's knee. "Quiet," he snapped. "Don't upset it."

Her scream cut off abruptly. The bison still stood there, staring at them with bloodred eyes, steam puffing out of his nostrils. His horns curved forward, and the tips looked razor sharp.

Sadie gave a sharp bark, and he reached back to run a hand over her head, hoping she'd stay quiet. Beside him, Frankie's breaths shuddered in and out, too fast. "Take a deep breath and hold it. Count to five and let it out."

He heard her breathe in, ending on a whimper, then she blew it out. "Again. I don't want you to pass out on me. I need you to keep Sadie quiet. She's pregnant, and I don't want her upset."

Frankie's breathing finally slowed down, and she murmured softly to the dog.

A bellow ripped through the cloudy morning, and the bison swung its massive head toward the departing herd. With one last look at Wyatt and Frankie, the animal shifted about and wandered across the valley toward the river.

"Oh, thank God," she murmured.

He faced the front windshield and put the car in gear, making sure all the bison were off the road, then continued to town.

By the time Wyatt pulled into a parking spot in front of the general store, Francine seemed totally fine.

"This is a charming little town," she said as she unbuckled her seat belt.

He looked up and down the street, saw the same old buildings that had always been there, just prettied up for the season. Neatly trimmed window boxes burst with fall foliage. Colorful flags announcing the harvest festival hung from the old-fashioned streetlights.

"Where do you need to go?" he asked.

"Children's clothing store."

"I don't think there's one here. But Marge might have something in the general store. That's where I'm going, anyway."

"Great, I can get clothes for John Allen, a rake and a horse blanket," she muttered just loud enough for him to hear.

"You can always order online from whatever fancy place you shop," he said and got out, letting Sadie follow behind him. She quirked a brow, and he wondered if this morning's tutoring session was making him snappy. Once again, it hadn't gone well.

"I just thought I'd get him some clothes to play in while we're here."

"Kade won't mind if Johnny keeps the ones we borrowed yesterday. Plenty more you can have."

She didn't say anything, but he could just imagine how pissed her father would be to know his grandson was wearing old hand-me-downs.

Wyatt opened the door to the general store and held it for her, and she walked by him at a fast pace, her heels clacking on the wood floor. "You might wanna look at getting some play clothes for yourself," he murmured.

Marge walked up to them just then. She was a staple in town and ran a tight ship, but she had the biggest heart ever. Maybe that was why she and his mother had been best friends. "Marge, this is Francine Wentworth, from New York City. She needs some jeans and stuff. Maybe even a horse blanket, too."

Francine rolled her eyes at him as she shook Marge's hand. "Hi, Marge. It's nice to meet you."

"Welcome to our town, Francine." Marge leaned in to hug him. "'Bout time you came to see me, Wyatt." She grabbed a handful of his hair. "You need a haircut."

"Yes, ma'am," he said. Almost thirty years old and she could still make him feel like a rebellious twelve-year-old.

"Come on, Francine. I'll show you around," Marge said.

He stayed put a minute, watching Marge and Frankie interact. They'd just met yet were already talking like old friends, even if they were polar opposites. Marge, with her curly silver hair and reading glasses hung around her neck, old jeans and a pressed shirt. Frankie and her perfectly done blond hair and makeup, fancy coat and black suit.

He looked around the store, the merchandise. Another place in town that hadn't changed over time. It always smelled the same in the general store—coffee, mothballs, penny candy, a wood-burning fire and new denim. Most days a group of older men sat by the stove and played checkers and gossiped.

He craned his neck to see the back of the store. Yup, three of them were back there, already in place. He winced—he'd have to pass them to get to what he needed. He and his friends had probably pranked—or worse—all of them at least once in his troubled youth.

He'd been to town a handful of times since coming home, tried to avoid locals when he did. No sense putting it off. He headed toward the kitchen supplies, and as he approached the checkers players, they all stopped talking. Wyatt nodded at them but didn't stop. As soon as he passed them, they started talking again, this time in whispers.

The price you paid for being a teen rebel in a small town.

He looked around to see where Francine was and saw Marge had shown her to the shelves full of folded jeans. They were still chatting, which surprised him. What would a big-city woman have to talk about that much with someone she'd just met in a small town in Montana?

He studied Francine, noting how her face lit up when she laughed. She seemed much more relaxed now. More like the Frankie he called her in his head.

Picking up the rest of the items he needed for the ranch, he then headed for the hat section. He picked one out for Johnny that matched his own.

He set it on the counter with his other items as Marge set down a stack of clothes for Francine. He noticed there were some women's jeans and shirts, even a hat and boots.

"Oh! I forgot a hat for John Allen," Frankie said, starting to walk away.

"I got him one," he said, pulling his wallet out.

She walked back to the counter and took it from his stack and laid it on hers. "Thanks."

He pulled it back. "I said, I got it."

"You don't need to do that."

"I want to."

She glanced at the price tag, and bit her lip. "It's kind of pricey for such a small hat."

A bitter taste coated his tongue, and his lip curled up. "I can afford it. I'm not the poor ranch hand your dad accuses me of being. I had fun with Johnny, and I want to get this for him. He's a great kid."

She held her hands up. "That's not what I meant at all. Sorry if I offended you… That's sweet of you. I know he'll love it."

They finished their transactions, and as they left the store, Wyatt's stomach growled. He stowed their packages in the back seat of the truck, then closed his door. "You want breakfast?"

"No, thanks. But I will have some coffee."

They entered the diner next door, and Sadie followed them in.

Frankie looked at him. "Are dogs allowed in the diner?"

He waved at one of the waitresses, then opened a screen door to another room. Sadie trotted in and immediately lay on one of the dog beds. "So many people bring their dogs to town, they have this room set up with food and water bowls and stuff."

She raised an eyebrow. "Very progressive for such a small town."

"We're not Podunkville," he bit out. "Just makes it easier for dog owners, and we don't have to leave them in vehicles."

"That's not what I— Never mind. Forget I said anything." She huffed.

They sat in a back booth, and Patsy, their waitress, stopped by for their order. "Coffee?" She held the pot up.

Francine nodded. "Please."

Patsy filled her cup, then turned to Wyatt. "You want the usual, honey?" she asked, filling his mug.

"Hey, Patsy. Yeah, thanks." He pushed the laminated menu across the table. "Sure you don't want something, Frankie? They have great food."

She smiled at Patsy. "No, thank you, I never eat breakfast. Just black coffee." She watched Patsy walk away, then looked at him. "You're not going to quit with the *Frankie*, are you?"

"Hasn't anyone ever called you that before?"

She shook her head. "Not even in school or on the playground."

"Francine just seems too formal for you when you're relaxed, laughing with Marge." He paused, took a sip of hot coffee. "Or covered in mud."

Her cheeks colored prettily, and her nose wrinkled.

"I'll stop calling you that."

She held up her hand. "No, it's okay. I kind of like it. Reminds me I need to relax more often. Just promise you won't do it in front of my colleagues."

Patsy returned and set his food down and refilled their coffees. His mouth watered when he saw she'd included one of the diner's famous cinnamon rolls.

He picked up his fork and glanced at Frankie.

"That roll is as big as my hand." She held her hand over the cinnamon roll. "Correction, it's as big as *your* hand."

"Yeah, and awesome." Even as he said it, she licked her lips, and he wanted to be the one to make her do that. Not a cinnamon roll. He cut a piece off and handed her his fork. "Just try it. One bite won't kill you."

She took the fork and slid it between her lips. Her eyes closed as she chewed. "That is the best thing I've ever eaten in my life."

He picked up her unopened bunch of silverware and took the napkin off. "Go on, have some more. I've got plenty here." He'd just taken a bite of eggs when she snatched a piece of bacon off his plate and ate it in no time.

"I thought you don't eat breakfast."

Red stole across her cheeks, and she looked sheepish. "Must be this mountain air. I'm actually hungry today. And I haven't had bacon in years."

He grinned, gestured to Patsy for another order, and slid his plate across the table to Frankie. "Well, don't deprive yourself anymore. Dig in."

They ate in near silence, and it surprised him that it was not an uncomfortable silence.

The front door opened, and a cold wind blew in two older women. They zeroed in on Wyatt and frowned. As they passed their table, one of them harrumphed and muttered the word *trouble*, and he almost spit out his coffee.

Frankie leaned forward toward him. "What on earth was that about?"

"Teachers."

"Yours?"

"Yup."

"I take it the school years were not pleasant ones?"

They weren't—especially with the passing of his mother. But the last thing he needed was her learning he'd never graduated. "Why?"

"Because they keep whispering to each other and looking at you. Do you want to leave?"

"Nope. It was a long time ago. Let's just say I wasn't the best student."

FRANCINE PUSHED OPEN the door and walked to where Wyatt waited for her. He leaned against the side of the truck, legs crossed in front of him, thumbs in his belt loops. He seemed to be staring at something and nothing at the same time, his mind a million miles away. The hint of grief on his face really surprised her.

She hated to bring him any more grief, but the conversation she'd just had in the diner bathroom troubled her. She dreaded bringing it up to Wyatt, but she had to, for John Allen's sake. Once they were on the way back to the ranch, she leaned forward and turned the radio down a bit.

"When I was in ladies' room, one of those old biddy teachers followed me in."

"And?"

"She told me to stay away from you, for my own sake. And safety."

His face turned to stone, and he wouldn't look at her. A muscle jumped in his cheek, and she all but heard him grinding his teeth. "That so?"

"She said you're a troublemaker."

He rolled his eyes. "I'm ashamed to admit it, but I was a bit of a rebel in my younger days."

"Just a bit?"

He winced. "Okay, more than a bit. I wasn't the best student, and I had a lot of anger."

"So you *were* in a gang?"

"What?"

"She said you'd been in a gang."

"I guess from her point of view, we were a gang. I hung around with a few guys and we had motorcycles, played pranks, caused trouble around town, if you call that a gang."

"You had a motorcycle in high school?"

He shrugged. "I did odd jobs for the mechanic in town. He let me buy an old one for cheap. Had to rebuild it from the frame up."

"You rebuilt a motorcycle as a kid?"

"I was always good with mechanics. Better than learning anything in school," he muttered almost under his breath, but she heard him. "Damn thing stalled more than it ran. But it was mine, and it got me off the ranch. I still have it, even though I don't ride it much anymore."

She steeled herself, dreading the next part, hating to pry, but she had to. "The old lady also said you'd been in jail."

His whole body went still, and his eyes narrowed. "This is why I hate coming to town," he muttered. "That part is true."

Adrenaline flooded her body, and she wanted to jump out of the truck. What had she been thinking yesterday, letting her boy spend the day with a complete stranger—who had a record!

"I'll bet she didn't tell you that I took the rap to keep my friend safe, did she?" he ground out through clenched teeth.

"No, she didn't. Is that what happened?"

"My friends and I were out one night. Todd had gotten hold of some booze, so we were passing the bottle around, feeling pretty good. He did something stupid and the cops were called. If his dad had found out, he'd have beaten Todd again, real bad. So I took the rap and had to spend the night in jail. The charges were dropped the next morning because someone saw what really happened and stepped forward."

He glanced over at her, a vein jumping in his temple. She could tell how much it bothered him to talk about this. She set a hand on his arm. "I'm sorry. I had to ask because of my son."

"I'd never hurt a kid," he ground out, yanking his arm from beneath her touch. "And I don't appreciate anyone thinking I would."

Chapter Five

Francine held John Allen's hand as they walked toward the barbecue dinner set up outside the main lodge. The night sky was full of stars twinkling like diamonds. A perfectly beautiful sight to end a not-so-perfect day.

Her mind immediately flashed to Wyatt, and she gave a brief shake of her head. She'd had a good time with him this morning. It was the first time in a while she'd spent time with a man she didn't work with, one who didn't want to use her for something else—like her ex. The weasel had only married her to gain a position at her dad's company and, apparently, to control her finances. After the divorce, Frankie had a tough time getting Robert to call John Allen or even write a birthday card.

Maybe that was why Wyatt was such a surprise. He wasn't who she'd thought he was originally—and she liked him. Finding out about that jail stint was a shock, but she liked him more, knowing he'd done it to protect a friend.

It made him more attractive, if that was even possible.

But the drive home had been very tense. She knew she'd upset him with her questions, and she'd tried to apologize once more, but he'd brushed her off. He'd been so quiet the rest of the way back that by the time he pulled up to the lodge, she'd worried he might not stop the truck completely. But he'd been a gentleman and opened her door for her, got her packages out of the back. Then he'd sped off with Sadie, practically leaving a trail of dust behind him.

She spotted him across the patio now, talking to a small group of men. Worn denim cupped his butt, contoured to his thigh muscles. His arms were folded across his chest, biceps bulging. She appreciated the view, just like she would any other man who filled out his clothes well—at least, that was what she told herself.

From the way they'd left off earlier, she guessed he wouldn't be speaking to her any time soon. Maybe he'd come around eventually, and she could avoid unwanted awkwardness during her stay.

The evening had turned even cooler, but there were so many fire pits and heaters around it made for a cozy space.

He turned as she watched him, and caught her eye. He dipped his head just a bit, then cocked a half grin and waved at her son.

She looked around at her coworkers and their families already seated at most of the tables. She and John Allen were running late because her father had almost had a coronary when he saw her dressed in her new jeans. He'd said that as his daughter, and an executive vice president in his company, she had to maintain a higher standard for herself, and that didn't include dressing like a cowgirl. She'd changed into a copper sweater, mink-brown pants and ankle boots to appease him.

And she felt ridiculous.

It was one thing to keep her dress code during business hours, but this was supposed to be a relaxing evening eating barbecue al fresco—not entertaining her father's guests in his Park Avenue mansion, or the estate in the Hamptons.

At least he hadn't thrown a fit about John Allen's new clothes. Wyatt had given her the hat to give to her son, and

John Allen had been overjoyed to get it. She bet anything he'd be sleeping with it.

They walked toward the dwindling line at the buffet tables and she picked up two plates.

Juggling them, she scooped up some salad for herself, then moved on, looking ahead to what might tempt John Allen.

"Hi," said a woman behind her. "Can I help you with one of those?"

Francine looked up to see a pregnant woman with long dark hair and a smile on her pretty face. "Not necessary, but thank you," she said, just as one of the plates tipped and food started to slide.

The woman grabbed for the other plate and averted a potentially embarrassing disaster. "I'm Kelsey Sullivan. Happy to help out."

"Sullivan?"

"Yup. I married Nash, the oldest of this motley crew of ranchers."

"I'm Francine Wentworth, and this is John Allen."

An older woman with blond hair and a pretty face walked over. "Hi, pumpkin," she said to Kelsey, giving her a one-armed hug, then held her hand out to Francine. "I'm Bunny Sullivan. I don't think we've met yet."

"Mom, this is Francine Wentworth, and her son, John Allen."

"It's nice to meet you, Mrs. Sullivan," Francine said, puzzled but trying not to show it.

Kelsey laughed. "Confusing, right? Bunny is my mother. I was Nash's physical therapist, and while I was working with him, she and Nash's dad fell in love. Then I fell for Nash." She shrugged. "Easy to do with these Sullivan men."

"You better believe it," Bunny said. "There aren't men

like this group anywhere else in the world. They'll happily lend a helping hand to whoever needs it, and welcome them in." She grinned. "Well, Francine, enjoy your stay. I'm sure we'll see each other again." She walked over to speak to another group of people.

Just then a little girl with long dark curly hair ran up to them and threw her arms around Kelsey's waist. "You're Johnny, right?" she asked, staring at John Allen.

"I'm John Allen Wentworth," he said, holding his hand out to the little girl.

"I'm Maddy. This is my mommy, and that's—" she pointed at one of the cowboys standing near Wyatt "—my new daddy."

"Hi, Maddy," Francine said, smiling.

The girl waved a hand at her. "Come on, Johnny, you can sit with me."

Her son beamed. "Mr. Wyatt calls me that."

"I know. My uncle says that's your name." She looked around. "Hey, I wanna meet your grampa, 'cause Uncle Wyatt says he has a big stick in the mud."

Francine snorted, then clapped a hand over her mouth. She could just imagine what Wyatt's real words had been.

"Madison! You know better than that. Now you apologize to Ms. Wentworth for saying something mean about her father," Kelsey said.

Maddy's eyes opened wide. "I'm sorry," she mumbled and dropped her head so her curls draped her face.

"It's okay, Maddy," Francine said. "I won't tell him."

"So, can Johnny sit with me at the kids' table? My cousins are there." She pointed at a smaller table next to Wyatt, indeed filled with four rough-and-tumble miniature Sullivan men.

Francine looked down at her son as he crowded against

her legs, staring at the table Maddy pointed to. She patted his shoulder. "Maybe later, Maddy."

Maddy shrugged. "Sure. See ya." She ran off to join her cousins.

John Allen stared after Maddy, then turned his head to look up at Francine. "Mommy, can I go sit with them?"

It took everything in her not to let her jaw drop. Her shy baby actually wanted to meet strangers? "Sure, honey. Want me to walk you over?"

"How about if I walk you both over and introduce you to the boys and their dads?" Kelsey asked, gesturing at the group of men talking to Wyatt.

Francine looked at her and mouthed her thanks. She finished filling a plate for John Allen, and they walked to the kids' table.

"Francine, this is my husband, Nash. And these are his brothers, Wyatt, Luke, Kade and Hunter." Kelsey pointed at each one as she introduced them. The men all nodded at Francine.

Wow. All five men wore denim, flannel Western shirts, cowboy hats and boots. Was it her imagination, or was testosterone wrapping around her like a warm blanket? Every one of them was rugged, solidly muscled and immensely attractive. Although her eyes kept going to Wyatt. There was just something about him…

"Frankie," Wyatt said, his voice a rumble that sent those damn traitorous tingles racing down her spine.

Kelsey glanced at her. "Frankie? Have you two met already?"

"Yeah, over some mud pies," he said, a half grin on his face.

Francine's cheeks heated, and she pulled at the neck of her suddenly too-hot sweater.

"You'll have to tell me that story some time," Kelsey said, looking between the two of them.

Wyatt squatted on his haunches. "Johnny, that hat looks awesome on you. You like it?"

"I love it! Thank you, Mr. Wyatt!" He threw his arms around Wyatt and squeezed.

Wyatt smiled, this time for real, and hugged her son back. "Good." He pointed at the other little boys at the table. "These are my nephews. Toby over there is nine, and is Kade's son. And these six-year-old look-alike monsters are Hunter's boys, Cody, Tripp and Eli. Boys, this is Johnny, and his mom, Frankie."

A chorus of *hey*s and *Hi, Miss Frankie*s filled the air, competing with the country song playing.

Maddy patted the bench next to her. "Come sit here."

Wyatt stood and plucked Johnny up, then swung him over the bench to sit next to Maddy. He took the plate from Francine and set it in front of her son, then bent over and whispered something to him.

He stood up and looked at her. "You want to come eat with us?" He indicated the table right next to the kids.

She nodded and sat on the wood bench, surprised when Wyatt dropped down next to her. She leaned closer and spoke over the loud music. "What did you say to John Allen?"

Wyatt tipped his head closer to her. "I told him to have fun, but if he wanted to come back and sit with you, we'd be right here."

A little spurt of warmth pinged her heart that he'd thought of her son's well-being.

"Thank you." She hesitated, then said, "You're a really nice guy, aren't you?"

He tugged his hat down lower, shadowing his face.

"Just don't let it get around. I have a rep to maintain." He scooped up a forkful of coleslaw.

She wondered why he hadn't been snatched up yet, like his brother Nash, but then, she'd already surmised he preferred to be alone. Which was a shame. Once you got past the prickly exterior and the bad-boy, leave-me-alone persona, he had a kind heart.

Wyatt leaned closer to her so she could hear him. "I'm riding out to check for stray cows tomorrow. Okay if Johnny comes with me, learns to ride a horse?"

His request darn near knocked her off her chair. Her gut instinct was to say no, but she looked at the next table to see Johnny laughing with the other kids, something he rarely did. She couldn't keep him wrapped in cotton batting forever. "Is it safe?"

"Yup. He can wear a helmet instead of a cowboy hat, and this first time, he'll ride with me. Thought I could show him some riding."

She glanced at him, studied his hazel eyes. "Why are you being so nice to John Allen?"

He shrugged. "He's a good kid. Funny. He's never been on a horse, has he?"

"No."

"Kids need fresh air, wide-open spaces. Adventure. Especially being cooped up in a city made of concrete."

"Wait a minute. It's not like I keep him in a cage in a concrete and steel building." She sent him a bemused look, then shrugged. "Besides, I grew up there, and I turned out okay. We go to Central Park—"

He raised his hands as if in surrender. "Didn't mean to put down your city. Just figured he might as well have fun, go exploring, while you're here. Besides, I don't want him wandering around the ranch alone."

She should say no. Keep the peace with her father during the merger—he was certain to blow a gasket. "Can I go, too?" The minute the words were out, she wanted to yank them back. She had a lot of work to do, but if she stayed up late and worked... She wasn't quite ready to let John Allen spend the day out in the wilderness with someone she hardly knew, even though something told her Wyatt would protect her son with his life.

"You sure the boss man won't mind?"

Leaning closer to his ear, she whispered, "Let's just not tell him. Deal?"

He turned just then, and they were kiss-distance apart. The sly grin slid off his face, and his eyes dipped to her mouth, studied it. She ran her tongue over her lips.

"You ever ridden?" He swallowed, hard.

Her mind flashed to riding him in a dark room, moonbeams bathing them in light and shadow. The traitorous tingles were back, rampaging now in her lower belly. She slid her eyes down to his lips—couldn't help it, really. Full and perfectly shaped— She reined in her imagination and asked, "A horse?"

He nodded, still staring at her.

"I took—" Her voice cracked, and she cleared her throat. "I took lessons years ago in school, and used to ride in Central Park before I had John Allen."

Wyatt Sullivan was dangerous. Dark, delicious—and she wanted him. Which surprised the hell out of her.

But she couldn't give in to those wants—needs...dark-of-night cravings.

WYATT BEAT HIMSELF up inside. What the hell just happened? They'd been talking about horses one minute, and the next, suddenly he'd been staring at those soft lips, wanting to take her back to his cabin and find out just how soft they were.

It was just a fantasy. No way would she go for a man like him. She was beautiful, smart, a real class act. He was a dropout who'd spent more time behind bars than he'd let on today. That was his own business, but if the obvious differences didn't make her run, learning about his time in Texas would. He might live and work on a luxury guest ranch, but it wasn't his way. She needed some rich guy to sweep her off her feet and keep her in the lifestyle she was familiar with.

He was black leather, dusty jeans and sweat-stained T-shirts, covered in muck, hay and engine grease. She was fancy shoes, pink suits and expensive jewelry, and she belonged on a pedestal.

A heavy hand clapped onto his shoulder, and he knew without looking it was his dad, and it was time to do the Sullivan Ranch duty.

"Evenin', everyone," Angus said. "Boys, the music's been playing awhile, but no one seems to want to dance. Can y'all get something started?"

Sure, he asked nicely, but in Angus-speak, it meant *get up and do your duty.*

Wyatt and his brothers all stood and nodded at the women. As he walked away, he heard Kelsey tell Frankie she was in for a treat.

He hated this part. Fact was, he stayed away from the guests as much as he could. He'd much rather be walking the land, fixing what needed fixing, tending to the animals—hell, even going on a week-long cattle drive just to avoid the guests who ran amok on the ranch. The cows and horses were much more his speed than these corporate types who came here to vacation.

Or work, he amended silently, glancing at Frankie still sitting at the table as he lined up with Luke, Kade and Hunter on the dance floor. Nash had said he wasn't ready yet to try dancing again. In that one way, Wyatt considered him lucky—well, not really, considering he had a leg injury, but it got him out of making a spectacle of himself up here in front of everyone.

Another song started, one they'd all practiced line dancing to. Pop swore it was the only way to break the ice with guests who were sometimes too shy or too intimidated to get up and have fun on the dance floor.

Wyatt didn't mind dancing, but he'd much rather it be one on one with a warm woman in his arms, alone in a sea of other couples on the floor who weren't watching every step he made.

He glanced at the table where his dad and Bunny sat and saw Frankie's father with them. He stared at his daughter across the rows of tables, then jerked his head.

Wyatt looked at Frankie, and she nodded, then stood up. His eyes followed her as she circulated among the guests—probably her coworkers and their families. *Guess she's doing the Wentworth duty now.*

The last couple she talked to sat closest to the dance floor, and when she was done, she looked up at him and his brothers, smiling a real smile this time. She watched him for a few minutes, and as ingrained as the steps were, he was afraid now would be the time he'd stumble over his feet, make an ass of himself in front of this sophisticated woman. He jerked his head, beckoning her to join them.

Her eyes widened, and she shook her head.

Come on, he mouthed silently.

She shrugged, shook her head again.

Just then Kelsey walked up next to her and grabbed her hand, pulling her along to the dance floor. They slid into place behind him and his brothers, where he assumed they watched the steps. The line dance turned them sideways, then backward, so she and Kelsey were in front of them now.

Frankie laughed as she stumbled over the steps, trying to watch Kelsey and look back at his steps to keep up.

Her laughter brightened her whole face, took her a little ways off the pedestal he'd imagined her on earlier.

Eventually a few other guests got up to join them, and soon everyone was laughing.

The music changed suddenly to a slower song, and he turned slightly, in time for Frankie to bump into him.

He held his hand out. "Dance?" he asked her, surprising himself.

She backed up a step and shook her head. "No, I have two left feet when it comes to any kind of dancing. Thanks, though."

"Aw, come on. I'll teach you how to two-step."

She hesitated, staring at his outstretched hand like it was a bear claw or something. Just as he was about to give up and drop it, she took his hand and stepped forward, then put her other hand on his shoulder. He'd danced this way many times—why now did the touch of her warm hand in his make his body tighten? He'd never known hands could be one of those zones people always mentioned when talking about sex.

"I'll apologize now for stepping on your toes," she whispered, just loud enough for him to hear.

He turned his mouth to her ear. "Don't worry about it, darlin'. My boots can handle it."

A tremor tumbled through her, and he wanted to continue whispering in her ear if that was what it took to make her feel something. He had a feeling she stuffed her feelings down deep, and it was a real shame.

The third time she stepped on his toes, she winced and

started pulling away. "See? I'm not any good at this. I'll just go sit with my son and you can find a better partner."

He kept his grip on her hand, pulling her back to him. "How 'bout we slow it down and just move to the music?"

She looked up at him, her blue eyes popped wide-open. Her gaze slowly dipped down his face, as if studying it, ending at his lips, and it shot sparks straight to his groin. He wanted to kiss her, right then and there, but he knew it would only give her trouble with her father and a reason for her coworkers to talk.

He knew he should stay away from her.

He knew he should stay away from her and her fancy suits and shoes.

He knew he should stay away from her and her cute kid.

But God help him, he couldn't stay away. And it scared the hell out of him.

Chapter Six

Francine drew even with Wyatt's solid black horse, Deacon, at the top of a small rise, and reined her chestnut to a stop. She glanced at him, holding her son perched in front of him on the horse, both staring straight ahead. "Why are we stopping?"

He gestured with a nod of his head. "Sunrise."

The sky filled with the most glorious colors—pinks, oranges, yellows, purples—and she was in awe. The sun tipped the rims of the sharp-edged mountains gold, and they stood out against the sky—majestic and grand reminders of how beautiful the countryside was. This was definitely worth the early hour, and now she felt bad for grumbling into her coffee.

"Amazing," she breathed, noticing the puffs of air coming from her mouth. "This beats the exercise bike and treadmill, reading emails and headlines this time of day," she joked.

Wyatt stared at her. "Do you always work?"

"No, not always," she said, annoyance—and maybe a little guilt—putting a snap to her words.

"Yes, you do," Johnny said, leaning forward from his perch on Wyatt's horse to look at her.

She caught a grimace on Wyatt's face just as he turned his head away.

"Well, your grandfather isn't going to let me run the company someday without hard work." She tugged her hat down a little lower on her head. "But I promise to try to spend more time with you."

Guilt pricked her insides. She'd been thinking about the new program the company was working on until Wyatt stopped his horse. Johnny—and when had she started calling her son Johnny?—rarely called her out about working so much. This was all she knew. She'd grown up spending time at her father's office—mostly because it was the only way she ever got to spend any time with him as he built his company from the ground up. It hit her hard that now she was doing the same thing to Johnny.

The sun crested over the mountain and illuminated Wyatt and Johnny on the stunning horse. She'd never seen a horse so black—his coat gleamed with iridescent jewel tones in the sunlight, much like the underside of a raven's wing.

Johnny giggled, that infectious sound that always made her heart ping with happiness, and she looked at him pointing up at an eagle. The predator rode the air current, searching the meadow for breakfast, soaring until it finally swooped down.

Her baby boy had already laughed more on this trip than he had the previous month at home.

And just what did that say about her as a parent?

"Hey, Frankie. You coming?"

Startled, she glanced up to see Wyatt's horse several yards away. She'd been so lost in thought she hadn't noticed they'd started up again. Clicking Molly to get her going, she noticed the easy way Wyatt sat on the horse. His body moved and flowed as Deacon walked across the meadow, almost as if they were one.

Never had she seen a man more at home on the back of

a horse. Or a more sensual one. Comfortable in his own skin, he exuded sex appeal without trying to. He was made for life out here on a ranch, at one with the land he lived and breathed.

How could he stand the isolation? Yes, his family lived here, and they had year-round guests. But still…

She looked around at the towering mountains, golden in the early morning. They curved and loomed as if protecting the land, protecting the Sullivans and their ranch, protecting all of the animals that made this place their home.

By the time the sun had risen high above them, she found herself enjoying the peace and quiet of the valley. No traffic rushing, no crowds jostling her, no constant sirens and horns. She found herself relaxing, really relaxing and letting go of work worries, for the first time in years.

And what surprised her even more was that she was having fun helping Wyatt spot cows that had wandered off alone. A couple of times ranch hands had ridden out to meet them and gather the strays to take back to the rest of the herd later on.

She'd worried that Johnny would get bored, but he was having the time of his life. Wyatt had been great about explaining the ins and outs of a working cattle ranch and answering all of her son's questions.

Throughout the morning, she'd made a point of taking pictures of the beautiful scenery, the cows and especially Johnny on the horse. Which meant Wyatt was included in some of them. But that couldn't be helped. Right?

One particular stunning view of the mountain covered in autumn-colored trees, with a silvery waterfall cutting a swath straight downward, had her stopping yet again to take photos. After she'd taken some from every angle, she looked up. Wyatt and Johnny were far ahead of her, almost specks on the horizon.

Rustling in the bushes to her left made her jump, and she peered closely to see what it was. A low mooing sound had her wheeling her horse around to where the sound came from.

She got off her horse, grabbed the rope looped around the saddle horn and walked cautiously toward the bushes. A cow's head appeared through a break in the foliage, and she slowly approached it. "Did you get lost?"

The cow mooed at her and tossed its head up and down.

She looked up to see where Wyatt was, but she didn't even see them now. Pulling out her cell phone, she noticed only one bar. She typed a quick text to Wyatt and hoped he would get it.

Walking around the bushes, she spotted the problem. The cow had her leg tangled up in some dry branches. Francine leaned forward to move the branches, but the cow kicked backward at her, and she had to jump to the side to avoid its hoof.

"Oh, come on. I just want to help you."

She walked forward again, and the cow kicked back, this time grazing her shin. She rubbed the throbbing spot with her hand. "Now cut that out. I'm not afraid of you," she said, hoping the words would convince herself as well as the cow.

The cow turned its head to stare at her, and while Francine had never seen an angry cow, this one was definitely pissed.

"You know what? My dad gets that same look on his face when Dow Jones takes a plunge. Now let me help, okay?" She walked closer again, a ball of fear rotating in her gut. The cows hadn't looked this big from the back of a horse. Sidling up next to the animal, she started to bend over, but the cow slammed into her and knocked her into the bushes.

She was momentarily winded but managed to catch her breath. "That does it." It was one thing to let her father run roughshod over her, but a whole different thing to let this stupid cow do it. She extricated herself from the dried branches and walked several feet away. As she brushed dead leaves off her clothes, she noticed a rip in her jeans and a hole in the sleeve of her brand-new denim jacket.

She grabbed the rope off the ground and stomped to the cow. "Now settle down, Bessie," she said, and slapped the cow's rump.

The cow swung its massive head around to give her a death glare.

Francine took advantage of the movement and got the rope around its neck.

Keeping as much room as she could between them, she pulled dry brush away, then worked to untangle the cow's leg. As soon as the cow was free, it mooed, and broke through the bushes.

Francine hurried around to try and catch it, but didn't need to worry. The cow had stopped next to Molly, and was munching on some grass. "You okay, sweetie?" Francine asked the cow, rubbing her hand along the smooth hide behind her neck.

The cow mooed again, then turned its head and swiped its tongue along Francine's right cheek. It took everything in her not to flinch at the warm slobber now coating her face.

"Oh…well, then. You're welcome," she said and stepped back. She waited until the cow went back to eating grass, then scrubbed her sleeve along her cheek. *Can a cow's feelings be hurt?* She didn't know, and she didn't want to find out. Then Francine rolled her eyes at herself and pulled a pack of wipes from her pocket to scrub her face. At least she hadn't worn much makeup today—since Bessie had just licked half of it off.

Now she had to hurry and catch up to Wyatt and Johnny. She picked up the trailing rope and started to remount her horse but noticed a cloud of dust on the horizon. A horse and rider emerged, galloping at a fast clip toward her.

"Frankie! Are you okay? What happened?" Wyatt shouted as soon as he came within earshot. He had one arm tucked around Johnny, holding him tight to his body.

"I found one of your lost cows."

Wyatt reined in his horse, then slid off. "Why didn't you wait for me? That cow could have killed you." He whispered the words so Johnny wouldn't hear, but they had the full force of angry cowboy.

"Poor thing had her leg caught in some dead branches. I had to help her." When he continued to scowl, she added, "I can take care of myself, you know. Been doing it for years now."

"You're a city girl. This is the wilderness. A wild animal could have been stalking that cow and would have gotten a buy one, get one free dinner with both of you. There are wolves out here, Frankie, and cougars, bison, bears."

"I'm fine," she said, her pride stinging. "And I don't need a lecture."

She started to walk away from him, but he grabbed her and bundled her into a hug. "You don't know what I was imagining—you out here all alone and lost." He squeezed her tighter, wrapping his big body almost around her, and she could honestly say she didn't mind one little bit.

"Did you think I was helpless?"

"Uh, yeah," Wyatt drawled in her ear, then finally let her go and stepped back.

"Mommy, you saved a cow?"

She beamed at her son, who was sitting atop the horse

just fine alone, she noticed. "I sure did. I couldn't leave her here all by herself."

"I'm proud of you, Frankie," Wyatt said. "Just don't ever do that again."

"Guess I'm not so bad for a city slicker, am I?" she asked him.

"You're okay in my book." He smiled, and his words sent a surge of warm pleasure through her chest.

He looked at her again, then gently cupped her chin and turned her face sideways. "You're hurt." He dug a hand-kerchief out of his pocket and dabbed at her cheek. "Not bleeding now, but you've got a scratch." He turned her face the other way. "Why is the other half of your face all red?"

"Oh. That. Bessie licked me when I got her out of the branches."

Wyatt stared at her a second, then he burst out laughing. She glared at him, but Johnny's little-boy giggles soon followed.

"I'm glad I can amuse you both so much," she said mildly and climbed back up on her horse. She cut around Wyatt and Johnny, towing Bessie behind her.

Wyatt and Johnny caught up to her before too long. "Head that way," he said, pointing toward the lake. "Johnny and I rounded up a few more cows and left them there. I've got more help coming out to take them back."

Just as he said the words, she saw a couple of cowboys were already there, leading the wayward cattle back to the ranch. She gratefully turned the rope over to one of them and said goodbye to her bovine charge. Watching as the two cowboys and their faithful dogs herded the cattle along, she wondered what it was like at roundup time, with hundreds of cattle being collected by all the cowboys.

Not that she'd be here to see it, but it would be cool. Loud and dusty, but exciting to see anyway.

She wheeled Molly around and followed Wyatt and Johnny, heading toward a sparkling blue lake.

Colorful rocks and gravel surrounded the body of water that went as far as the eye could see. Tall reeds and grasses swayed in the breeze at their end of the shore.

"The water is so clear. Is it all like that?"

Wyatt nodded. "Pretty much all over the ranch. I've seen rowboats out there that look like they're hovering over the water instead of sitting on it. Swimming in it is great—you can see everything real clear." He leaned closer to her. "Makes for some fun skinny-dipping," he whispered.

Her cheeks went blistering hot, and she couldn't get the image of him swimming naked in the lake out of her head. *Oh, God.*

He reined his horse to a stop under a tree and slid off. He tied the reins to a branch, then lifted Johnny down. She walked her horse under the tree as well and dismounted. Wyatt took the reins from her and tied Molly off, making sure the horses could access grass and water.

She unbuttoned her jacket and took it off. "Day really warmed up, didn't it?"

"Yup," he said, pulling things out of his saddlebags. He spread a red-and-white-checkered cloth on the ground, then set out food.

"You brought a picnic?"

"Mrs. Green. She runs the lodge kitchen with an iron oven mitt and a big heart. Woman can't stand to see anyone not eating."

Francine spied fried chicken in one container. Normally she stayed away from fried foods, but the sight of the golden-fried deliciousness made her mouth water. He opened other containers and set plates by each of them, along with plastic utensils and napkins.

Just as Johnny was reaching for a chicken leg, she

snatched his hand. "Hold on, young man. You know the rules. You've had your hands all over that horse and who knows what else today."

Johnny sat back and held his hands out, palms up.

She pulled the packet of sanitary wipes out of her jacket pocket and took one out, then cleaned his hands with it. Glancing up, she saw Wyatt watching her, a piece of crispy fried chicken halfway to his mouth. She dropped her chin and looked at him, one eyebrow raised, as if daring him to ignore her rule.

He rolled his eyes but set the chicken on his plate and held his hands toward her.

She held the packet of wipes out to him, but he shook his head, moved his hands closer to her. *Seriously?*

She pulled another wipe out of the packet, then proceeded to clean his hands.

His very large hands.

His very large, manly hands.

Hands she tried to ignore as she wiped every bit of them clean.

Hands that she wanted all over her body.

"I think they're clean now," Wyatt said in that deep, rough voice that shot arrows straight to her girlie bits.

Shoving the dirty wipes in the saddlebag, she fought to keep the heat from her cheeks, wished it would snow or something. Anything to cool her body after having something so innocent as cleaning hands turn into something so intimate.

She fixed a plate for Johnny, then herself, needing some time before she could risk looking at Wyatt again.

Honestly, what was wrong with her? He was *so* not the type of man who had ever attracted her. She liked men clean-cut, suit and tie, executive office—*boring*, her conscience shouted in her head.

Wyatt was the opposite—long hair, untucked shirt, dusty cowboy boots and a constant five o'clock shadow. The whole thing put together made for one hell of a sexy, mouthwatering man.

Wyatt said something to Johnny, pointing at the lake. She followed their gaze to see an enormous moose with huge antlers sprouting from its head walk out of the brush not too far from where they were picnicking. She swore it was as big as, if not bigger than, a pickup truck. Following behind him were another moose with no antlers and a younger moose.

"Mommy, look! Mooses!"

"Shh, sweetie. We don't want to scare them." She tried to keep the fear out of her voice, didn't want to alarm her son. While Johnny's gaze was still pinned to the moose family at the edge of the lake, she shifted to stretch out behind him and reach over to tug on Wyatt's sleeve.

Wyatt turned to look at her, and her mouth went dry. Every move he made was sensual. Even when he didn't mean to, it was part of him, what made him so attractive to her. Heck, to any woman, she was sure.

He bent over her, that long dark hair framing his face, and God help her, she wanted him to kiss her.

"What?" he whispered, his eyes dropping to her mouth.

"Um…" Great, now her brain wasn't functioning. "Moose," she whispered, pointing at them.

He cracked a grin. "Yes, Frankie. Moose."

Her synapses finally kicked back in. "I mean, are we too close? Will they charge us?"

"As long as we're quiet and don't make sudden moves, we'll be fine. It's rare for them to be out this time of day. Must be hungry or thirsty."

Even as he said the words, the big moose wandered into the water until he was shoulder-deep in the lake, then dipped his head. The water turned his coat an even richer dark brown. The young moose pressed close to the other one, then dipped its head to drink water at the shore.

"Why is that big one in the water so deep?"

"That's the male, a bull moose. He's scooping up plants from the bottom of the lake to eat."

Johnny turned to look at her and Wyatt. "Look! They're a family, just like us! A daddy, a mommy and a kid."

A COUPLE HOURS LATER, Johnny's words still echoed in Wyatt's head. *A family.* Something he'd never really given much thought to. 'Course, he'd never found anyone he wanted to spend the rest of his life with. Shocked and very surprised, he had to admit the kid had wormed his way deep into Wyatt's heart.

But Frankie. She was so far out of his league. Beautiful, smart, dedicated and a good mother, even though she worked way too many hours.

For one thing, she was some big executive in her dad's company. Woman worked almost 24-7. In fact, they'd had to hurry back so Frankie could clean up and get to the afternoon meeting. Johnny had begged to stay with him the rest of the day, and Wyatt had been surprised she'd agreed, after making sure he was okay with it.

He and Johnny had spent the afternoon in the horse barn. He'd taught Johnny how to take care of the horses after being ridden. Then they'd mucked out stalls and repaired tack, and he had to admit it was a lot more fun doing the unending chores of a working ranch with Johnny keeping him company.

Late afternoon, they headed back to Wyatt's place. He and Johnny stopped by Frankie's room on the way to grab a bag of stuff to keep the kid entertained. But they didn't end up needing it. Johnny kept up a constant chatter about everything they had seen and done on the ride that morning, and then about getting the horses settled in clean stalls. By evening, Johnny was yawning so much it looked like his head was going to split open. Good thing Frankie had given permission for her son to stay until she picked him up later.

He got Johnny settled on the couch, then saw the kid holding a book. "Will you read to me, Mr. Wyatt?"

Wyatt held very still, dread churning acid in his stomach. "I need to get some work done. Why don't you read it?"

Johnny yawned again. "No, you read to me. Please?"

Now how could he refuse that cute face blinking sleepily up at him? He sat down on the couch, and Johnny scooted next to him. Flipping through the book, Wyatt noticed there weren't a lot of pictures, but definitely lots of words. *So* not what he needed.

He flipped to the first page with pictures and thought a minute, then started making up a story.

"Hey, that's not how it goes," Johnny interrupted him, pointing at the first line.

"You sure?"

Johnny nodded. "Yup. It's my favoritest book of all."

"Haven't you ever made up different stories to go with the pictures? We could try that, if you want."

Johnny looked up at him, his mouth quirked in a frown just like his mom's. Then he yawned again. "Okay."

Wyatt had to think fast to keep the kid entertained until Johnny's head finally drooped, and he fell asleep. Getting up from the couch, Wyatt moved quietly so as not to wake Johnny, then pulled a throw over him.

As he passed the kitchen table, he knocked an envelope onto the floor. He picked it up, but really wanted to chuck it out the door. It was the details of his GED test. He opened it slowly, hoping he'd read the name wrong the night before. He traced a finger over the line affirming who his exam proctor would be. *Miss Bromfield.*

Old biddy number one, the one who'd most likely told Frankie about his past in high school. Hell, she'd probably gotten a kick out of talking about his bad reputation back then, and the night he'd spent in jail.

Of all the teachers he'd ever had, and the ones who taught in town now, why couldn't it be one of them proctoring the GED test he'd signed up for?

But no.

His luck it had to be the one teacher who hated him the most, who never gave him an inch or extra time to complete assignments. She hadn't cared when he'd told her he had trouble reading.

Now, when it mattered, when he was ready to do something about getting his GED, *she* had to be the one person whose help he needed.

He'd just have to work extra hard and get it over with fast.

A beep from his back pocket sounded, and he pulled his phone out. A text from Frankie.

Mtg running over. Okay for JA to stay longer?

He sent a text back to her. No prob.

He grinned at her response. UR the best.

He looked over at Johnny, still sleeping on the couch, and decided to go over his lesson plans. He grabbed a beer and settled at the kitchen table.

SEVERAL HOURS LATER, a knock sounded at the door. He got up and opened it to a yawning Frankie, leather tote bag in hand. "Hey. You look exhausted," he said, opening the door wider. "How'd you get here?"

"I am," she said, covering her mouth over another yawn. "One of your brothers dropped me off." She stepped into the cabin, and he noticed her shirt was half untucked from her navy slacks. Even the thin blue stripes on her white shirt seemed wilted. "Where's Johnny?"

"I put him in the guest room."

"I'm so sorry I'm late. Did you two have dinner?"

"Yep."

He heard a growl and realized it was coming from Frankie.

She blushed and slapped a hand to her stomach.

"I guess you didn't have dinner?"

"I wasn't hungry. I just wanted to get finished for the day."

"Want a sandwich?"

"I'd love one, if it's no bother."

"No bother at all."

"Thank you." She set down her bag. "I'm going to go check on Johnny. Be right back." And she walked in the direction he pointed for the guest rooms. He'd woken Johnny from his nap to eat, then settled the boy into the guest room.

He made a turkey sandwich for Frankie, adding chips to the plate just as she walked back into the living room.

"He's sound asleep. Sadie is curled up right next to him."

"How many pictures did you take?"

"None," she said and fiddled with one of her cuffs.

He just looked at her.

"Okay, about fifteen. Maybe twenty." She spread her hands wide. "Hey, I can't help it," she said and smiled.

He grinned, jerked his chin toward the couch. "Sit down

and relax. Almost done here. Want something to drink? I've got iced tea, soda—"

"Beer?"

She kept surprising him. He grabbed a beer from the fridge, popped the top and took everything to her. She sat ramrod straight on the couch, hands folded in her lap.

"I told you to relax."

"I am," she said, looking up at him like he was dumb or something, her mouth quirked.

"Yeah, right." He set the plate and beer on the old coffee table, pulled her high heels off, and swung her legs up onto the couch. "This is how you relax at my place. House rules." Grabbing a couple of throw pillows, he set them behind her back, then handed her the beer. "Drink."

She stared at him as he sat at the other end of the couch, then tilted the bottle to her lips and drank. "Oh, God, that's good. Icy cold." She started to set the bottle down on the table. "Coaster?"

He took the bottle from her and plunked it on the old wooden coffee table, then handed her the plate. "Eat."

She saluted him. "Yessir." She leaned back, balancing the plate as she bit into the sandwich. She finished chewing and swallowed. "Wow. Best. Sandwich. Ever."

He felt, rather than saw, her feet flexing on the sofa cushion next to him. Having seen the torture devices she wore every day, it was a wonder her feet didn't bleed or fall off. Going on instinct, he reached for one of her feet and set it on his lap.

"What are you doing?" she mumbled around a bite of sandwich, trying to yank her foot back.

He held on to it. "Helping you relax after a long day."

"You don't need to do that."

He pushed his thumbs into her arch, rubbing out the aches.

She moaned. "But don't let me stop you."

Her moan did things, and he wanted to rub a lot more. Why was he doing this? She was a guest, her and her son. It wasn't like she'd be staying any longer than the two weeks her father had booked for the retreat. *Don't get involved. She's way out of your league, dumb ass.*

She set the plate on the table and sank back against the pillows. He set her foot down gently, then pulled the other one onto his lap. He'd never had a thing for feet, but Frankie's were pretty, with the hot-pink polish on her delicate toes.

He heard deep breathing and glanced up to see she'd fallen asleep.

Great. Wake her and Johnny up, drive them to the lodge, get them upstairs? Or put her in the third bedroom and she could get that much more sleep.

The dark shadows under her eyes made the decision for him. Her face was pale, making the scratch on her cheek stand out.

He'd been scared shitless when he realized that morning Frankie wasn't with him and Johnny. Images of her being attacked by a wild animal had flashed through his mind, one after the other, until he couldn't stand it. Then he'd seen her with that damn cow, so proud of herself, dust covered, scratched, her clothes torn and cheek bloody.

He'd wanted to take her in his arms and never let go, which scared the ever-loving hell out of him.

So instead he'd yelled at her.

He stood and went to his bedroom for a T-shirt, set it on the bed in the other room. He checked the guest bath and made sure it was stocked.

Walking back into the main room, he stood next to the couch, then gently touched Frankie's shoulder. "Hey, you need to go to bed."

She groaned and turned her face into the back of the couch.

He bent over and picked her up, and she snuggled into his arms, tucked her face into his neck. His body hardened instantly, and he wanted to carry her to his own bed. *Dangerous territory here.*

He entered the guest room and set her gently on the bed. Eyes barely open, she latched her arms around his neck before he could back away and pulled him down. She kissed him and sighed, her lips warm and soft, tempting him beyond belief. He cupped her cheeks but wouldn't let himself touch her anywhere else when she wasn't fully awake.

"Hey," he whispered. "Frankie."

Her eyes opened wide, and she scanned the bed, the room, then his face. "What are you doing?"

"Trying to be a gentleman right now." He pulled her arms from around his neck and stepped back. "You need to sleep."

"I've got to get Johnny and go back to the lodge." She tried to stand, and he gently shoved her back down.

"You're exhausted. He's sound asleep, and you're about there. Take the extra time and sleep here. You can even lock the door if you don't trust me." He grinned.

She looked up at him, her face so serious. "I do trust you."

Her words shook him to the bottoms of his boots. He didn't think anyone had ever said that to him. "I left a T-shirt for you," he said, hating the rasp in his voice. "Bathroom is through there. Get some sleep."

He forced himself to turn away and close the door before he gave in to need and begged her to let him stay.

Chapter Seven

The next morning, Francine woke up and stretched. The black cotton T-shirt she wore was old, washed so many times it felt soft as silk, and she snuggled it up to her nose. Wyatt's faint scent clung to the material, and she inhaled. *Maybe he won't notice if it's missing?*

She'd slept like the dead and felt great. Glancing at the clock, she noted it was still early, not even six. The meeting today didn't start until eight, so she had time to wake Johnny and head up to the lodge in time to get ready... and before her father or anyone else noticed she and her son hadn't spent the night in their suite.

She snuggled under the green comforter decorated with a moose border, content to lie still for just a few minutes more. Glancing around the guest room, she noted the simple, rustic furnishings. A cozy nook had a bay window and a window seat with pillows dressed in dark greens and browns. She'd love to curl up there with a steaming cup of tea and a good book. *Yeah, in what spare time?*

Big wooden beams crisscrossed the ceiling. It all lent itself to a very warm and comfortable room, one she liked even more than her suite at the lodge. A stone fireplace sat opposite the bed, firewood laid in—all she'd have to do was strike a match and light it. The room was the complete opposite of her modern high-rise apartment in the city.

For the first time in a long time, she actually felt relaxed.

A painting rested on the mantel over the fireplace. A snowy scene in the woods, with a few trees casting long shadows across the white snow. She got up to study it more closely and felt the isolation depicted, sensed there was a lot of underlying meaning in it.

Was that how she felt, what she'd experienced since her separation and divorce? Maybe because she was so isolated and insulated at work.

She looked for the name of the artist, but it only had the letters *KS* in the lower corner. Maybe she could ask Wyatt, or up at the lodge, who the artist was. She'd love to see more of his or her work.

Wandering to the window, she peeked out the curtains and saw the crystal-clear blue lake Wyatt's cabin bordered. "What a gorgeous setting," she murmured. The lake was so calm today she could see the mountains and trees reflected like a mirror in it.

A huge elk stepped out of the trees not ten yards from where she watched. His dark brown coat was thick, burnished by the sunrise, and he had an impressive set of antlers on his head.

Laughing to herself, she wondered if deer and elk compared antlers the way men compared cars and other stuff.

She took advantage of the brand-new toothbrush on the sink in the guest bath and freshened up, then dressed in her clothes from the previous day.

As much as she hated to leave her cozy nest, she had to head back to the lodge and get ready for the day. Opening the solid wood door, she headed down the short hallway.

Walking into the open living space, she realized she'd been so tired the night before she'd missed the gorgeous view through the floor-to-ceiling windows. Even better than the view from her room.

Turning toward the kitchen, she noticed another gorgeous view—Wyatt stood at the stove, a hand towel slung over his shoulder, cooking something. She hadn't paid attention to the gourmet's dream kitchen that opened into the living room. Gleaming stainless appliances, granite countertops, rich wood cabinets and a rough stone archway framed the stove. She wasn't much of a cook, but even she coveted this kitchen.

Johnny sat at the kitchen table coloring. He looked up at her and grinned. "Hi, Mommy."

"Morning, sweet pea," she said and walked over to kiss the top of his head.

She inhaled, then followed her nose around the island.

"Good morning," she said.

Wyatt glanced up from the stove top. "Morning. Sleep okay?"

"Mmm, great. Best sleep I've had in a long time. Thank you for putting both of us up." Scanning the room again, she said, "I hadn't noticed last night what a big cabin this is. Does someone else live here with you?"

"Nope. I picked this one for the view…and the kitchen."

She inhaled again. "Whatever you're cooking smells amazing. I mean, that sandwich last night was fabulous—much more than just turkey slapped on two pieces of bread. Did you take cooking lessons somewhere?"

He shrugged. "I picked it up here and there. Coffee's on the counter," he said, gesturing with a spatula.

She turned around and saw a blue stoneware mug sitting next to a coffeepot on the granite countertop. After filling her cup, she took a sip, and her eyes popped open. "This is the best coffee I've ever had."

"Even in New York?"

She took another sip. "Surprisingly, yes. Even in New York."

He didn't respond to her, but as he reached for a plate, she could have sworn there was a grin on his full, sexy lips.

"What's your secret?"

He shook his head. "Can't tell you," he said, making his voice low and mysterious. He jerked his chin at the table. "Grab a seat. Breakfast is ready."

She sat at the round wood table, and he followed her, setting a plate brimming with food in front of her and a smaller portion in front of Johnny. Eggs, hash browns, biscuits and gravy, bacon.

"Do you eat this way every day?"

"Nah."

"So you did this just for us?"

He shrugged. "Dig in before it gets cold." He brought another plate to the table and sat down with them.

She dug in to the biscuits and gravy, and it was heaven. "I'm going to go home with forty extra pounds," she said and took another bite.

"Mommy, we're not leaving now, are we?" Johnny asked, a frown marring his normally cherubic face.

"Not yet. We still have a while yet. Do you like it here on the ranch?"

"I love it. I want to be a cowboy when I grow up."

Wyatt grinned, and ruffled his hair. "You'd be a great cowboy."

Johnny beamed at him, and she was a bit disconcerted to see the hero worship shining in her son's eyes as he looked at Wyatt.

Wyatt was great, but they'd be leaving soon. Johnny would return to life in New York—fewer cowboys, more being groomed to work at her father's company someday.

For some reason, that thought made her pause now. Would Johnny want that life, the way she had?

Wyatt leaned closer to Johnny. "And your mom here… I think her new name should be Frankie Wentworth, cow wrangler. You agree?"

Johnny laughed so hard he almost fell off the chair. "Yeah! Now she needs a badge with a big cow on it."

Francine drained the last of her coffee and got up. "Need more coffee?" she asked, ignoring their laughter, and walked around the counter to the coffeepot. As she headed back to the table with the pot, her elbow hit a stack of books sitting on the end of the counter, and they fell to the floor. Papers scattered everywhere.

She set the pot on the counter and knelt down to pick everything up. She reached for one volume that appeared to be a textbook.

"Leave it. I'll get it," Wyatt said and brushed by her to pick up the books and papers.

The tone of his voice surprised her, and she moved out of his way. "I'm sorry, Wyatt."

"No big deal," he said, but he shoved everything in a kitchen cabinet. He turned to face her and checked his watch. "Don't mean to rush you, but I need to head out and get the workday started."

"We'll get out of your way." She packed up the items Johnny had taken out of his backpack.

"I'll drop you off at the lodge on my way out." Wyatt walked to a cabinet and pulled out a travel mug emblazoned with the Sullivan Ranch logo, then filled it with what remained in the coffeepot. "Take this with you," he said and handed it to her.

"That's not necessary."

"It'll just get poured out otherwise."

"Can I go to work with you today, Mr. Wyatt?" Johnny asked.

Wyatt ruffled Johnny's hair. "Not today, pal. I've got a boring meeting with my dad and brothers, then have a day full of even more boring chores."

"Oh," Johnny said and looked down at his boots.

The mama bear in her crawled up her throat. It was one thing to brush her off—quite another to hurt her son, especially when he'd initiated this bonding by continuing to invite Johnny out. For the first time ever, Johnny had reached out to someone other than herself. She opened her mouth to respond, then Wyatt surprised her by squatting down next to Johnny.

"If you and your mom don't have plans tonight, you should go to the bonfire."

"What's a bonfire?"

"We make a really big fire and toast marshmallows and make s'mores."

"What's a *suhmore*?"

Wyatt turned his head up and looked at her, then back at Johnny. "You've never had s'mores? They're the best dessert ever invented. Graham crackers, marshmallows and chocolate, all smashed together. Sound good?"

Johnny scuffed his boot along the wood floor. "Will you be there?"

"You bet I will. I have to teach you how to toast marshmallows, don't I?"

Johnny grinned. "Yay!"

Wyatt stood up. "Then it's a date."

"Mind if I tag along on your date?" she asked.

"Sure thing," Wyatt said.

They headed outside, got in his truck, and he pulled out onto the road lined with trees full of gold, red and orange fall leaves. As they neared the lodge, the pink sports car she'd seen the other morning headed toward them. Wyatt raised his fingers off the steering wheel and waved at the driver. The car sped past them, toward the cabins scattered around the lake.

They reached the lodge, and Wyatt pulled in to the circular driveway in front of the main doors. He got out and opened the passenger door for her and Johnny. "Well, see you tonight."

"Thanks for putting us up, and for making us breakfast," she said, brushing a hand on his arm when he started to walk away.

"Anytime," he said, then rounded the truck.

She and Johnny walked up the few steps to the lodge, but something made her pause and turn around. Wyatt slammed his door, then raced down the driveway and got on the road. Had she done something to offend him? She thought back over the morning. He'd seemed fine, up until she knocked the books off the counter, then he'd practically shut down.

Maybe it was something else.

She tamped down on her insecurities. Wyatt was nothing like her lying ex-husband.

Right?

FRANCINE HUFFED OUT a breath. The last thing she wanted right now was to be around a lot of people, especially since most of the guests at the ranch were her coworkers. The meetings that day had not gone well, and more than one angry voice had been raised in discussions, especially her father's.

But she couldn't let Johnny down, not when he'd been especially good about staying at day care and not sneaking out. She'd ordered room service for their dinner to give her some space, and now it was time for the bonfire.

Bundled up in sweaters and coats, they made their way to the gathering. The big fire was already going, snapping and crackling against the cool night. She stopped at the edge of the patio and looked around for open seats. Someone waved to her, and she realized it was Kelsey. Taking Johnny's hand, she walked with him over to say hello.

"Hi, Francine. Hey, Johnny. You want to join us?" Kelsey asked.

"We'd love to, thanks." Francine got them settled, then looked around for Wyatt. Nowhere to be found.

Kelsey leaned closer to her. "Looking for someone?"

Embarrassed, and feeling like a fifteen-year-old looking around for the captain of the football team, she shook her head.

"He's on bonfire duty."

"Who is?" Francine asked.

"Weren't you looking for Wyatt?"

"He—uh—he promised Johnny he'd show us how to toast marshmallows."

Kelsey grinned and nodded. "Sure."

Francine's cheeks heated, and she was grateful for the fire to blame it on.

Kelsey's daughter, Maddy, jumped up and stood in front of Johnny. "You need a s'more bag. Come on. Race ya!" She and Johnny took off for one of the tables at the edge of the patio.

"The kids are all having a sleepover tomorrow night. Think Johnny would want to join them?" Kelsey asked.

"A sleepover? Where will it be?" Francine asked, then chewed on the inside of her cheek. Johnny hadn't ever slept over at anyone's house.

"It'll be at our cabin, with Maddy, Kade's son, Toby, and the triples. We'll play games, pop some popcorn, maybe watch movies."

"Who or what are the triples?"

Kelsey laughed. "That's what Toby called Hunter's triplets when they were born, and it kind of stuck. What do
you think about the sleepover?"

"It's so nice of you to ask. I'm fine with it, if Johnny
wants to."

Johnny and Maddy ran back to them, holding little
paper sacks. "Mommy! Can I go to Maddy's tomorrow
night?" He was all but jumping up and down, waiting for
her to answer.

She looked at Kelsey. "I guess there's your answer."
She pulled her son back down onto the bench. "You'll all
have so much fun." He was growing up so fast, and now
he actually wanted to go play with other kids.

Snuggling him close, trying to hold on to her baby just
a little longer, she looked around the bonfire. Last night
was about mixing and mingling. Tonight was about families sitting together, toasting marshmallows. It was times
like this, seeing other families—whole families—that hurt
her heart. Johnny was growing up without a father, since
her ex was an SOB who never paid attention to him. Her
own mother had left her and her father behind long ago,
so she knew what it was like to be missing a parent. Even
now, it was rare for Francine to get a Christmas or birthday card from her mother.

"Mommy, do all daddies know how to make *suhmores*?"

She looked down at him as he stared around at the
groups of families. "I don't know, sweetie."

"I guess that's why I don't know how to make them,"
he said, his voice quiet.

And right there, she wanted to bawl. He didn't mention
his father very often. Knew somehow, instinctively, that
his father wasn't interested in being a dad. *The selfish,
son of a bitch weasel.*

As good as she was at her job, she felt like a complete failure when it came to family dynamics.

"There's my cowboy." Wyatt's voice drifted down, and he sat in the open spot next to them. "Did you eat all the s'mores without me?"

Johnny laughed, but she'd caught a sheen of tears in her baby's eyes. "Naw. We got stuff right here," Johnny said and held up the paper bags.

Wyatt handed them each a stick and showed them how to put marshmallows on the ends. "Now you hold it close to the fire. But not too close, or it'll get all black and yucky."

"Like the cookies Mommy made?"

"Hey, that was supposed to be a secret," she said and tickled Johnny until he giggled.

Wyatt's laugh rumbled, and he smoothed a hand over Johnny's head. No one else had ever gotten her son to open up socially like Wyatt had.

For just one second, she imagined them as a family, like Johnny had said. The three of them.

No. It could never happen.

Could it?

Chapter Eight

The next evening, Wyatt opened the door to his dad's office. His brothers had beaten him there, and their dad sat
behind the huge mahogany desk that he called his com-
mand center.

*Sure, where he sits and commands everyone and ev-
erything.*

"Boys, thanks for coming up here so late. I know you
want to get home after a long day."

All Wyatt had wanted after work was to go back to his
place and spend the evening with a beer and a ball game.
Kade's text about the meeting had shot that idea to hell.

"We need to decide what to do about finding a foreman
replacement for Shorty. He and his wife will be leaving
before too long."

Wyatt leaned against the table by the wall, kept quiet.
He wanted that job but knew Pop would never even give
him a chance.

His brothers all looked at each other and nodded.

"We all agree who it should be. Shorty's already given
his blessing, too. Don't have to place an ad or anything.
He'll be great at the job," Nash said.

"Who?" Angus asked.

"Wyatt," Nash said.

Wyatt whipped his head sideways to look at Nash. His brothers all thought *he* should get the job?

"Why him?" Angus asked.

Wyatt's pulse sped up, and his muscles tightened, dread churning a hole in his gut.

"Who do you think stepped in, picked up the majority of the load the last few months, what with Shorty getting ready to leave?" Kade asked.

Pop looked at Wyatt, a scowl on his face. "You want this job?"

"Yes."

"What makes you think you're qualified?"

"I know this place inside and out. I know what needs to be done. I know the land."

Angus leaned back in his chair, studied him. "How do I know you won't get mad and quit, hightail it outta here again?"

"This is my home," Wyatt said.

"And all you boys agree about this?" He looked at Nash, Kade, Hunter and Luke in turn as each nodded. "Clear out. I want to talk to Wyatt."

His brothers all filed out, and Hunter knuckle bumped him in support. Wyatt moved forward and sat in the chair across from his dad.

"I want to know up front if you think you can do this job."

"I've been doing it the last several months."

"I know physically you can do it. There's also a lot of paperwork to being a foreman. Hiring hands, payroll, scheduling, arranging cattle drives. I want Hunter to set up databases for the breeding programs, both cattle and horse. Foreman will have to manage it, keep it updated."

Wyatt's hands clenched around the arms of his chair.

It wouldn't do any good to blow his top now. He knew where this was going.

"You still have trouble reading, son?"

"Yeah, I'm still dyslexic. Not something you grow out of. But it is something you can learn to live with, compensate for. No one listened when I was young and having trouble. Now I can do something about it."

Pop's eyebrows shot up.

"At least now I can put a name to it."

Angus leaned back and steepled his fingers together. "That's good. I gotta tell you that most of the foremen around the neighboring ranches have college degrees, or at least a two-year associate's degree. You need to earn this job. I won't just give it to you because you're my son."

Wyatt took a breath, forced himself not to lose his temper. "I plan on getting my GED. Been studying." He stood, started to walk to the door, stopped. "One thing at a time, Pop. I want this job."

"Are you going to get in trouble again?"

Wyatt closed his eyes, the crushing weight of his pop's disappointment a palpable presence in the room.

"Have you seen me get into trouble lately?"

"Trouble has either followed you around, or you led the rebellion, since you were a kid."

"Well, I'm not a kid anymore. I had to grow up fast, take care of myself. I don't want trouble. I've turned my life around, and it's time you realized it."

"Time will tell," Pop said.

Wyatt turned and walked out, forcing himself to not slam the door. It could have gone better, could have gone worse. As his dad said, time would tell, and no one could make up Pop's mind but him.

He left the lodge and headed toward the barn to get his

motorcycle and go home. Raised voices in the evening shadows made his steps slow. Frankie and her father.

"Francine, you're spending way too much time with that ranch hand and not enough time working," Wentworth said.

"That's not true, and you know it. I put in longer hours than anyone else on this team. And he's not a ranch hand."

"What about two days ago? You and John Allen went off riding horses and chasing cows. That's beneath you. And then you spent the night at his cabin?"

"That's none of your business—"

"None of my business? People are talking, Francine. You're a Wentworth, and so is your son, and I won't have anyone muddying your name or position. The team needs to respect their VPs if this merger is going to be a success."

"I've earned that EVP title, you know I have," Frankie said quietly. "And we didn't spend the night as you're implying. He was watching Johnny for me, I went to pick him up and fell asleep—"

"He's not the right man for you. He'll end up hurting you and John Allen."

Wyatt's whole body stiffened, and an intense heat flashed through his chest. He had to get out of there before he punched Wentworth in his shiny silver Colonel Sanders beard. He almost ran down the path, but he kicked a stray rock and it clanged against one of the metal railings.

"Who's there?" Wentworth demanded.

"Wyatt? Is that you? Wait!" Frankie said, her voice getting fainter the faster he walked.

The barn in sight, he headed straight for his motorcycle and got on. He kick-started it, deciding he needed a long ride to cool off. First his pop had no faith in him, now Wentworth was sure he'd hurt his daughter. He'd had enough of fathers who ruled anyone and everyone with an iron fist.

"Will you wait a minute?" Frankie asked, appearing out of the shadows at a fast pace.

"I gotta go. 'Night, Frankie."

She grabbed his arm, wouldn't let go when he tried to pull away. "Where are you going?"

"Out."

"Can't we at least talk? I know you overheard, and I'm really sorr—"

"Drop it." He revved the engine, itching to feel the night air and the isolation of the open road.

"Fine," she said, then shocked him by climbing on the bike behind him.

"What're you doing? Get the hell off my bike," he said.

"Not unless you agree to stay here so we can talk."

"Not in the mood," he snapped.

"Then I'll go with you till you *get* in the mood."

Oh, hell. "Where's Johnny?"

"At a sleepover with your niece and nephews."

"You ever ridden on one of these?"

"Uh, no."

He revved the engine again, flipped up the kickstand. "Then hold on."

They took off like a shot, and she squealed, grabbing for his arms.

"Put your arms around my waist," he shouted.

Her arms slid around his stomach, and she squeezed.

"It's open road for the most part, but lean into the turns."

"What?"

"Just feel what my body does and do that."

He felt her scoot closer to him, molding her body to his.

Oh, crap. This might not be such a good idea.

It took her a while, but she finally seemed to get the

hang of riding with him. Only problem was, her body was doing things to his it shouldn't be. And the thoughts he was having about sleeping with her would never—could never—be a reality.

The sun had set a while ago, and now stars were popping out like diamonds in the dusky sky. This was the time of day he liked best, but it was marred by Wentworth's words. He felt like he was sixteen again, when fathers pulled their daughters out of his way or slammed the door in his face.

Yeah, he'd been trouble. But that wasn't him any longer. At least he was working on it.

Wyatt knew he wasn't the right man for Frankie. They were too different. So why did she turn him on so damn much? Every time she looked at him with those pretty blue eyes, he wanted to kiss her. When she laughed, he wanted to snatch her away to the closest bed—hell, any horizontal surface would do—and make love to her.

And if she pressed herself any closer to him on the bike, he'd embarrass himself like a thirteen-year-old boy with his first girlie magazine.

He spotted the turnoff to the old hunting cabin and took a right, bumping down the rutted road.

Space.

He needed a few minutes of space away from her.

She'd be fine at the cabin while he cooled off.

He drove into the grove of trees protecting the cabin and stopped the bike. "I'll be back in a few minutes. Go on in the cabin out of the cold."

He started walking away, but he heard her fancy shoes crunching on the dry leaves behind him.

"Where are you going?"

"I'll be back," he said and kept going.

She grabbed his arm. "Can I come with you?"

His patience snapped and he turned around, got up in her face. "I just spent the last thirty minutes with you pressing your smokin'-hot body against my back. Unless you want to take this into the cabin and get serious, I need some *space*."

Her jaw dropped. Then she snapped it shut and smiled. But it wasn't her normal smile. This one…this one was a siren's smile. One that said *come on in, let me show you a good time, sailor.*

"You think my body's smoking hot?" she asked and wrapped her arms around his neck.

He gripped her slim hips, tried to push her back. But she tightened her hold, pressed herself to him.

"I think you're pretty hot yourself, cowboy," she whispered in his ear.

His body hardened even more, bordering on pain.

"Frankie, I'm warning you—"

"I'm a single, healthy woman, standing in front of the most ruggedly attractive man I've ever seen, and he's just told me he finds me hot. What do you think I want to do now? Wait here like a good little girl while you go cool off?" She shook her head slowly. "Not by a long shot, cowboy."

She closed the short distance and pressed her lips to his. Her mouth fused to his, nipping, biting, licking, until it drove him damn near crazy. He thought his head—hell, his whole body—would explode from the sheer pleasure of her mouth.

He let go of her hips, slid one hand up to her neck and held her still while he took over the kiss. He cupped her ass with his other hand, pressed her against him until she whimpered. He walked her backward until they hit the cabin porch steps, then lifted her till she wrapped her legs around his hips.

She writhed in his arms, rubbing her body against his, and he stumbled up the stairs, kicked the door open. The cabin was dark, and he felt for the electric lantern on the table by the door, flicked it on.

A low glow chased some of the shadows away, enough to make sure the cabin was empty. He fumbled for the door, slammed it shut.

She circled her hips against his groin, and his knees almost buckled. He turned around, pressed her up against the door. She lowered her legs but kept full-body contact.

"You drive me crazy, Frankie."

He didn't think—no, he *knew* no woman had ever affected him like this. He'd never been a saint, but he'd always avoided relationships that went beyond some fun.

But with Frankie, it was more than that. Along she'd come with her kid, both worming their way under his skin. He *liked* being around them. It frustrated him, pissed him off—

She popped the top snap on his flannel shirt. "Now what was that you mentioned about getting serious?" She gripped his shirt and yanked it open.

Cool air hit his back as she pushed his shirt and jacket off. She stared at his upper body, then licked her lips.

It was all the invitation he needed. He pushed her thick blue sweater up until he could yank it off. Her light blue lace bra outlined her perky breasts, and he thought if he couldn't see her naked soon, he'd die. But God help him, he couldn't move.

She pushed off the door and stepped closer to him, reaching for the zipper on his jeans. The sound echoed in the quiet cabin as she lowered it.

"Wait," he said, his voice harsh.

"Why?"

"Are you sure about this?"

She nodded, slid her hand inside his jeans and touched him.

Then he really did almost explode. "I don't want to take advantage of you."

She smiled, that damn siren smile. "Seeing as how you're not even touching me—yet—I'd say I'm the one taking advantage of you."

"You're kinda bossy, aren't you?"

"You should hear what they call me in the boardroom."

Her words were light, but the hurt was there, beneath them.

"I don't want to hurt you."

"I'm tougher than I look."

"That's not what I mea—"

"I know what you mean." Even as he watched, a mask covered her face, and she kissed him, pulled him close. "Take me to bed, Wyatt."

He slowly unhooked her pants and let them slide down her long legs. She kicked off her shoes, stepped away from the pile of clothing.

He'd never wanted any woman this way, this much. He shucked his boots and jeans as she slid her bra off.

They reached for each other at the same time, hands sliding, exploring, taunting, teasing, seducing. The bed was old, just a twin size. She lay down and pulled him on top of her. The old iron frame creaked and groaned, but he didn't care.

He just wanted this vibrant woman beneath him with an insane passion.

He made himself stop thinking—stop thinking this was a mistake, stop thinking he'd eventually hurt her, stop thinking about the world outside—and just let himself feel.

FRANCINE WOKE WITH a start, a warm weight pressing against her backside. Wyatt spooned her from behind, one arm tucked around her middle, keeping her close. 'Course there wasn't much room to spread out in this tiny bed, in this tiny cabin. Their cocoon.

She looked around the one-room cabin, noted it was hardly big enough for a stove, table and two chairs, and the bed. And it was surprisingly clean for being out in the middle of God only knew where.

She couldn't believe what she'd done tonight. She'd gone on pure instinct when she climbed on the back of his bike earlier that evening. Then to actually seduce him? She'd never done that, even when she was married. Of course, Wyatt was nothing like her ex-husband.

Nor was he like any other man she'd ever met.

Maybe being in Montana was making her bolder, more adventurous in life.

He'd made her feel things she'd never felt before. The weasel had always told her she was frigid, that she never satisfied him.

But with Wyatt—well, they'd more than satisfied each other.

"You all right?" Wyatt's voice rumbled in her ear.

"Yes. You?"

He stroked his thumb lazily across her breast. "Yep."

"You're a man of few words, aren't you?"

"Don't think it's necessary to use a lot of words to get the point across."

"I forgot to ask where Sadie is. Is she at your cabin?"

"She's over at Luke's with her husband."

She turned her head to look at him. "Excuse me? Your dog has a husband?"

He grimaced. "Dang. That slipped out. Sounds goofy, don't it? Maddy heard us talking that Luke's dog is the father of her puppies and demanded the dogs get married."

She laughed. "That's the sweetest thing I've ever heard. Were you the ring bearer?" she teased.

"I walked Sadie down the aisle, seeing as Maddy said I'm Sadie's dad."

"Okay, now *that's* the sweetest thing I've ever heard. I want to see pictures."

"You would," he murmured.

She moved her arm to link fingers with him and caught a glimpse of her watch. A few minutes after eleven. "Oh, no!" She sat up fast, knocking his chin with her shoulder.

"Ow," he said and rubbed his chin.

"I'm sorry. I need to check on Johnny. He's never slept over with any kids." She flung the blanket off and the cold air hit her hard, making her skin prickle.

"Never?" he asked, reaching for his jeans on the floor.

"No." She leaned forward and picked up her clothes, shook out the slacks. "Oh, no. My phone isn't here." She scrubbed a hand over her face. "I must have left it in the conference room. We need to leave." She slid her slacks on, then pulled the sweater on, and stuffed her bra in her pocket.

"Take a breath, Frankie."

"But—"

A ding echoed in the tiny cabin, and Wyatt held his phone up. "I just texted Nash. He said Johnny's fine. They're having fun. Nash grilled burgers, made Johnny's new favorite dessert, *suhmores*, they played a rousing game of Candy Land—Maddy's favorite game—and watched *Cars*."

Relief hit her hard. She'd been frantic, worrying about what a rotten mother she was, having fun with Wyatt while her son was possibly crying for her.

She looked down at Wyatt, still naked, comfortable in his nakedness.

He looked up at her, the strangest expression on his face. Then he seemed to shake it off and linked his fingers with hers, brought her hand to his lips and kissed her palm. "Lemme get dressed and we'll go."

He swung his legs over the edge of the bed and stood, then dressed quickly.

She wavered, hating to leave but wanting to be closer to Johnny, just in case.

Wyatt picked up his denim jacket and held it out for her.

"No, you keep it. I've got this sweater on."

"I'll be fine. Wind's blowing." He held it for her to slip into, and she knew better than to argue this time.

"Thanks."

He pulled the jacket into place, buttoned it up and stood the collar up to protect her neck. Then he pulled her into his arms, pressed a kiss to her forehead. Pulling back, he looked into her eyes. "Come home with me?"

She studied his face. The words were simple, straightforward, with a touch of vulnerability coating them.

Leaning forward, she kissed his lips. "Okay."

They left the warmth of the cabin, and she shivered in the wind blowing through the trees. Full dark now, but the moon shone brightly, and the stars—the stars made her catch her breath.

"It's so beautiful out here."

"Yeah. I missed the nights the most."

"I thought you had always lived here."

The silence stretched out for several seconds.

"I was gone for a few years."

"Where'd you go?"

They'd reached his bike, and he climbed on. "South. Come on. Need to get back."

She climbed on behind him and wrapped her arms around his middle, knew better than to press the issue now.

But it raised some questions.

Everyone had secrets, times in their life they didn't want to discuss.

As they drove away, she wondered if he'd ever open up to her.

Chapter Nine

Francine had almost gone into an alternate state on the ride back to the lodge. She'd been content to hold on to Wyatt, feeling his body as he maneuvered the bike down the long, lonely stretch of road, the night air whipping against her face. She wanted to make love with him again but wasn't sure she'd have the courage to be the seductress this time.

She looked up when he stopped the bike by the path to the lodge. Her heart sank. Was he already kicking her metaphorically out of his bed?

"You want to run up and get your phone? So you have it with you?"

Okay, so maybe he's not tired of me yet. "Thanks. Be right back." She hopped off and hurried up the path and into the lodge. Sure enough, her phone was on the conference room table.

The lodge was quiet as she headed back outside. As she walked down the path, she heard a muted voice. Wyatt climbed off his bike and set the kickstand.

"Frankie, I need to go. Luke needs me in the calving barn."

"Is everything okay?"

"Cow having trouble giving birth. Luke needs a few extra hands. I'm sorry."

Luke was the veterinarian, she remembered. "Anything I can do?"

He looked at her, his mouth cocked up in half a grin.

She waved her hands. "I know, I know. Stupid question coming from a city girl."

He kissed her cheek. "Sweet of you to ask. You better get some sleep."

And with that, he was gone, almost running to one of the many barns silhouetted against the night sky.

Knowing she needed sleep to be fresh for the meeting the next day, she still found herself following the path Wyatt had taken. She peered through the half-open door spilling light onto the concrete, followed the light to the left corner of the cavernous barn. She stepped over the threshold, making sure to keep her steps quiet, and moved closer to a stack of hay bales so she could see.

Luke looked up from his position by the cow's rump and saw her, a flash of surprise crossing his face. He nodded at her, then went back to whatever it was he was doing.

Wyatt squatted next to Luke and they talked, then Wyatt got up and moved to sit next to the cow.

The cow jerked, letting out the most pitiful moo Francine had ever heard in her life. Wyatt's hands stroked the cow's side. He leaned closer toward the cow's head, and she thought he was talking to it.

Then she realized he was singing to the cow. His voice was low, gravelly, like the smoothest chocolate with a bite of the finest whiskey.

And utterly breathtaking.

The cow seemed to settle, laying her head on the ground. Wyatt leaned closer, keeping up the long strokes on her side.

Luke said something, and she tore her gaze away from

Wyatt. The vet was pulling on long plastic gloves—so long they almost reached his shoulders.

She blanched, realizing what would come next. Sure enough, he was reaching inside the cow, who jerked again, raising her head. Wyatt stopped singing and laid his hands on the cow's side.

She automatically moved forward to kneel next to the cow's head. "It's okay, sweet girl. They'll take care of you."

"Frankie, what're you doing here?" Wyatt asked in a low voice, squinting at her.

She stroked the cow's head. "Sing some more. It's keeping her calm."

He shook his head but started singing again.

Sure enough, the cow quieted down, but Francine kept stroking her head, just as mesmerized by his voice as the cow seemed to be.

Not quite five minutes later, Luke gave a grunt and guided a baby cow—a calf, she amended—free from its mother. "Looks like we have a boy," he said and grinned at her.

"Congratulations, Mama," Francine said, her voice breaking into a small sob.

"You okay?" Wyatt asked.

She swiped a tear off her cheek. "Birth is always a miracle, isn't it?"

Wyatt grinned, but Luke spoke up. "It will be if this little guy pulls through."

"What do you mean?" she asked, alarmed.

"Calving usually happens in the spring. We'll have to keep him warm and with his mother through the winter," Luke explained.

"How did this happen?" she asked, worried about the calf, praying he'd grow big and strong.

"Lucky the bull got out of his pen, and…well…got lucky one night."

Her cheeks burned, then went scorching when she caught Wyatt's gaze, and he winked at her.

"Thank you—both of you—for your help. My assistant is almost here, so you two can take off," Luke said, wiping his hands on a rag.

"I didn't do much. It was Wyatt's singing."

"Nah," Wyatt said. "Call if you need anything," he said to Luke, then held the door for her.

She and Wyatt walked outside, the lights from the barn illuminating the path. "I didn't know you could sing," she said, keeping her voice quiet.

"I don't."

"I just heard you—"

"That's nothing."

She put her hand on his arm to halt his progress. "It's not nothing. You have an amazing voice. Have you ever thought about singing for a living?"

"No."

"You're so talented. A voice like yours should be shared."

Wyatt looked up at the sky filled with stars. "Used to sing for my mom. She'd be real sick from chemo, said it was the only thing that made her feel better."

"I'm sorry. I didn't know she'd been sick. She must have been proud of you. I'm sure she'd want you to share your gift."

"Not interested."

She started to say something, but a huge yawn took over, and she covered her mouth, embarrassed.

Wyatt pulled her into his arms. "You should head on up to bed. It's nearly one a.m., and you need some sleep."

She lowered her head to his shoulder, slid her arms

around his waist. Knowing he was right didn't help. Sleeping next to him—or not sleeping—was all she wanted to do.

"'Night, Wyatt," she whispered, and forced herself to pull away.

"Frankie." He stopped her, then held her against his hard body, tilted her head up and kissed her so thoroughly her toes curled, and she swore she saw fireworks behind her closed eyelids.

He lifted his head and stepped back, but kept a hand on her till she was steady.

Forcing one foot in front of the other, she resolutely followed the path to the lodge, but turned back at the door. He was right where she'd left him, watching her. She waved at him, even though she couldn't see his face in the dark, then went inside.

He'd knocked her normal, safe, boring world on its axis, and she wasn't sure that was such a bad thing.

Chapter Ten

Francine woke up out of a sound sleep, the remnants of a delicious dream she'd been having about Wyatt lingering on her mind. She rolled over and muscles she hadn't used in a long time—a really long time—protested. Reality set in, and she remembered the time they'd spent in the cabin the evening before.

Did she have any regrets?

She looked at the clock and decided to think about it later. She could either go back to sleep for an hour or go for a walk, something she used to do but hadn't for a long time. Since Johnny was still at the sleepover, she decided to use the energy filling her body for the walk and clear her head.

She dressed quickly in her new jeans and sneakers, pulled on a thick jacket, and headed out of the lodge, just in time for sunrise. Earbuds on, favorite playlist set on shuffle, she stretched for a few minutes, then set off at an easy pace.

The morning came alive around her as she walked on the path around the lake. But it was still so early she hadn't encountered another soul. She rounded a corner and noticed a familiar lakeside cabin.

Wyatt's.

She grinned to herself, thinking she could just drop

by for a surprise visit. Or a little bit of early-morning lovema—

She stopped dead in her tracks.

The cotton candy–pink sports car she'd spotted a few times racing along the ranch roads sat next to Wyatt's truck, gleaming like a beacon in the early-morning sun.

She couldn't imagine any of his brothers driving a pink car. Maybe it was Kelsey's? While she was debating whether to turn back or continue on, his cabin door opened. Instinct driving her, she stepped off the path and behind a tree.

A life-size Barbie doll walked out the door. Long blond hair pulled back in a ponytail, which Francine swore bounced when she walked, big boobs, a tiny waist, tight jeans—pink, of course—and a matching pink puffy jacket.

Wyatt followed the woman—hell, girl—out to her car. Barbie shifted a couple of books in her arm and reached out to give him a one-armed hug. He didn't respond, kept his hands on his hips, but he didn't shove her away, either.

Francine clenched her teeth so hard she was afraid they'd soon be nothing more than enamel dust. A burning sensation started in her stomach, spreading up through her chest until it almost consumed her, making it hard to breathe.

She stepped backward, but a branch snapped, the crack echoing like a gunshot in the quiet morning.

Wyatt turned her direction and seemed to look right at her, eyes squinting, his mouth—the mouth she'd kissed over and over the night before—quirked in a frown.

She turned around and flat out ran back the way she came. She wasn't sure, but she thought he called her name.

Putting on a burst of speed, she tried to outrun the intense feeling of betrayal, of not being enough. She passed the lodge but couldn't face anyone at the moment, so she kept running, down the path and around the outbuildings.

If her pink suit and shoes hadn't already been ruined that first day, she'd have burned them on principle. Right then and there, she swore she'd never buy anything pink again.

Her chest heaved, and she finally had to stop. Her blind run had taken her to the corral, and she walked over to the wood fence. Leaning against it, she watched a couple of horses run and play in the grassy circle. She tried to slow her breathing so she wouldn't hyperventilate. Tears clogged her throat, making it hard to inhale.

Was Barbie with the pink car the reason he'd decided not to take her back to his cabin the night before?

She'd thought Wyatt was different than her scumbag ex.

What was wrong with her?

It was getting late, and she had to get back, get ready for the day. As she reached the circular drive in front of the lodge, the soft roar of an engine sounded behind her, and she glanced around.

Wyatt's truck.

She ran up the few steps to the front door, desperate to avoid him.

"Mommy." Johnny's voice calling her finally penetrated the fog in her head.

She turned around and saw Wyatt lifting Johnny out of his truck. Now she *couldn't* avoid him.

"Mornin', Frankie," Wyatt said.

"Hi, sweetie," she said, kneeling down to hug her son. "Did you have fun last night?"

He nodded. "It was *so* much fun!"

"Well, you can tell me all about it when we get upstairs." She stood up. "Thank you for picking him up," she said, forcing herself not to look up at Wyatt.

"No problem. I thought before day care he might want to see the calf born last night."

"Oh. Sure. That's fine."

Wyatt and Johnny started walking down the path to the cattle barn, then Wyatt turned around, held a hand out to her. "You coming?"

"Come on, Mommy!" No hope now of escaping to her room.

She pasted a smile on her face and joined them, stuffing her hands in her pockets. They entered the barn and walked to the pen housing the cow and her calf.

Wyatt lifted Johnny up so he could see over the gate. "Your mom helped deliver that calf last night."

Johnny turned his head to look at her, his eyes as big as fifty-cent pieces. "You did? Wow."

"I didn't do anything. Mr. Luke and Mr. Wyatt did all the work." She held on to the top of the gate and looked over the top at the sweet brown calf as he nuzzled his mother.

Wyatt set his hand on top of hers where it rested on the wood slat. "Don't sell yourself short. You helped calm her down."

She frowned, looked sideways at him, and moved her hand from beneath his.

He met her gaze, confusion in his eyes. "Hey, Johnny, stay here a minute and watch the calf for me, okay?" He set her son on the ground, and he peered through the slats at the cows.

Wyatt took her hand, wouldn't let go when she tried to take it back, and led her to the other side of the barn.

"What's up, Frankie? Something wrong?"

"No. Why do you ask?"

"I thought we had something special last night. Now you can't stand the sight of me."

"Is that what you tell all the women you sleep with?" she asked, hating the tears in her voice.

"What? I haven't been with anyone 'cept you in a long time."

She scrubbed her hands over her face. "I saw her this morning, Wyatt. Don't give me that."

"Who?"

"Teen Barbie with the pink car. Coming out of your cabin practically at the crack of dawn."

"Heather?" His eyes shifted away from her, then back, a poker expression on his face. "Remember the other day you knocked those books off the counter at my cabin?"

"Yes."

"She's helping me study for a big test I'm taking in a few weeks."

"At six in the morning?"

"She lives on a ranch nearby, and she's a teacher in town. She comes over early to go over lessons, then heads on to school afterward." He brushed a lock of her hair off her cheek.

"I'm sorry."

"For what? Thinking your dad was right, and that I'm going to hurt you? I don't play around on women." He cupped her chin, looked so deep into her eyes she swore he could see her soul.

"I'm sorry," she said again, ashamed of herself for doubting his integrity.

Wyatt looked over his shoulder at her son, then gave her a fast kiss, his lips igniting a fire in her lower belly.

She'd taken a leap of faith the night before, and again just now.

She just hoped she didn't live to regret it.

WYATT DIVED INTO WORK, morning blending into late afternoon, but Frankie was never far from his thoughts. It still bothered him that she had thought he could leave her the night before, then have another woman over. He'd almost been tempted to tell her what Heather was tutoring him on, but it was a matter of pride.

A brilliant businesswoman, Frankie had worked her way up in her father's company. He still found it hard to believe she was attracted to him. What would a woman with a master's in business want to do with a guy like him who hadn't finished high school? Who'd been called lazy and stupid growing up?

Which was why he'd decided to buckle down and do what it took to cope with his learning disability and get his GED.

He knew this—whatever it was with Frankie—wouldn't last. It couldn't. Frankie had a life in New York—one that would afford Johnny the best opportunities and education available. They deserved that kind of life. Besides, her father would never allow it. Any day now, she'd wake up and realize she was staging her own little rebellion by seeing Wyatt. Then she'd hightail it back to New York, and that would be it. He'd be left with the memory of her, the feel of her skin, the way she sighed and moaned in his arms—

A shout outside the barn caught his attention, followed by a scream.

He ran out the door and looked for the source. Another shout drew his attention to the patio near the lodge door. An older man held on to a teenage girl's arm, and a teen boy in full black leather stood in front of him, fists clenched.

"Is this who you've been sneaking off to see?" the man yelled at the girl.

"I'm sixteen and I can see who I want!" she screamed at him. She tried to pull away again, the fringe on her brown jacket swinging wildly.

Yep. Father and daughter.

Wyatt thought he recognized the man as one of Frankie's coworkers.

The boy held out his hand to her. "Come on, let's go."

She tried to shake her dad's arm off and yank free, but he gripped it tighter.

Wyatt worried this would escalate. He shot a quick text to Frankie, and another to Kade.

Voices and tempers raised louder and higher, and he knew he had to step in. He started to walk over to them just as the boy lunged forward, shoving the dad backward till he let go of his daughter's arm.

The sound of sobbing reached Wyatt, and he looked around. Johnny was crouched next to a wrought iron chair, crying. He must have sneaked out of day care again.

He ran toward Johnny just as Kade ran up the path, with Nash following as fast as he could, talking on the phone.

"Sheriff's on the way," Nash said as he passed Wyatt.

Wyatt reached Johnny and picked him up. "You okay, bud? Are you hurt?"

Johnny threw his arms around Wyatt's neck, clutching him tight. "They scared me."

Wyatt rubbed his back, trying to calm him down.

The door opened, and Frankie and her father ran outside.

"What happened?" she asked, stroking Johnny's hair.

"Is my grandson hurt?" Wentworth demanded, his face pale.

"He's fine. I think he got scared by the yelling." Wyatt gestured to the argument just as the boy shoved the older man again, and this time he fell. The man got up and lunged at the boy.

Frankie gasped. "Peter!"

Kade and Nash separated them, keeping them from fighting any more. The sheriff's vehicle and another police cruiser pulled into the circular drive, lights flashing. Sheriff Wolfe got out of his car, and two deputies hurried out of the second car. They split up and took over holding the teen boy and Pete.

The hypnotic strobing of the red and blue lights made Wyatt dizzy. The saliva ran in his mouth, and he thought he'd be sick.

"What's going on, folks?" the sheriff asked, one hand on the butt of his weapon. He glanced at Wyatt, narrowed his eyes.

Great. He'd had plenty of run-ins with Sheriff Wolfe when he was a rebellious teen. His vision tunneled, and spots danced in front of his eyes. He needed to get out of there.

He started to hand Johnny to Frankie, but the teenage girl burst into tears and ran to Frankie's side, nearly knocking her over.

"Ms. Wentworth, help me."

Frankie wrapped an arm around her shoulder. "It's okay, Layla. We'll get this straightened out."

"I'll take Johnny inside," Wyatt said and started to turn around.

"You need to stay here," the sheriff said.

Ice skittered along the back of his neck.

The lodge door opened, and Kelsey and Pop walked outside. "Hey, Johnny. You want to come inside and have cookies and milk with Maddy?" Kelsey asked.

"That sounds good, bud. You'll love Mrs. Green's cookies."

Johnny nodded, and Wyatt set him down. Kelsey took his hand and led him inside.

Pop moved forward. "Why don't we all go inside and straighten this out." He tilted his head toward the small crowd that had gathered. He led the way inside to one of the private sitting rooms at the side of the main room.

One of the deputies passed by Wyatt, and the odor of cigarette smoke, stale coffee and jail wafted off him. The breath backed up in Wyatt's lungs, and he swallowed hard against the bile rising in his throat. He stayed by the door, ready to escape as soon as he could.

"Who wants to start?" Wolfe asked.

Pete, Layla and the boy all spoke up at once.

The sheriff raised his hands, then pointed at Kade. "You start."

Kade shook his head. "Wyatt was first on scene. I came out when he texted me."

Wolfe focused his attention on Wyatt, and the weight of his stare made his stomach heave. He focused on not puking in front of everyone, then felt a hand grip his. Frankie stepped closer to him, silently supporting him. He held tight to her hand, grateful.

"I was in the barn and heard shouting. I went outside and saw Peter arguing with that boy."

The kid sneered. "I ain't a boy, I'm a man."

Wolfe glanced at him, his expression speaking volumes. "Pipe down, Brady."

At least that glare wasn't focused on Wyatt today, and he stood a little taller. "Looked like Layla wanted to go off with Brady, and her father was trying to stop her. Then Brady shoved Peter, Peter shoved back, Brady pushed him down. Then you pulled up."

Sheriff Wolfe turned to Pete. "You're not from around here?"

Peter shook his head. "I'm from New York, here with the Wentworths." He nodded to Allen Wentworth and Frankie. "Layla's my daughter. I brought her with me while her mother—my ex-wife—is in Europe."

Wolfe turned toward Layla. "How did you meet Brady?"

"I went into town with a couple other kids, and we met at the movies."

"I didn't know about this, Sheriff. If I had, I'd have put a stop to it long ago. You can see he's not the right boy for my daughter."

The words echoed in Wyatt's head. How many times had he heard those words? He studied Brady. The anger seemed to waft off the teenager in waves.

Just like Wyatt at that age.

"Can I go now, Sheriff?" Wyatt asked.

Wolfe's eyes slitted as he looked toward Wyatt, followed by a half turn of his head. He jerked his chin toward the door.

Wyatt gripped the doorknob, whispered to Frankie he would check on Johnny. He escaped the sitting room, finally able to take a deep breath.

On his way to the kitchen, he swung into the restroom and splashed water on his face. He looked at himself in the mirror, trying to see if he was still that rebel teen covering up a learning disability, and grief over his mom, with anger and attitude. Trying to see if he was that defeated convict in a Texas prison.

He gripped the marble counter, leaned closer to the mirror, looked himself in the eye.

The doorknob rattled, and he jerked. He dried his hands, opened the door for the guest waiting outside and moved out of the way. His boots echoed as he walked through the big lobby toward the smaller kitchen the family used.

He pushed the door open and saw Kelsey and Maddy sitting with Johnny at a quiet table in the corner.

Wyatt barely got past the doorway when Johnny saw him and jumped up, running full tilt toward him, cookie in one hand. Wyatt swung him up into a hug, every protective instinct making him hold tight.

"Everything okay?" Kelsey asked in a low voice.

"Fill you in later." He sat in the vacated chair, Johnny on his lap, and picked up a napkin to wipe the milk mustache off the kid's face. "You liking those cookies?"

Johnny nodded. "Yup."

Wyatt took one off the plate. "I can't resist Mrs. Green's chocolate chip cookies." He took a huge bite, made an exaggerated moan and rubbed his stomach. "Mmm, good."

Johnny smiled, but Wyatt could tell it was an effort.

Poor kid. He shouldn't have seen what just happened outside.

"You wanna play a game?" Maddy piped up. "Grampa has a bunch here for us."

Johnny shook his head, then laid it on Wyatt's shoulder.

Kelsey stood. "Maddy, we should get home, get your daddy his dinner."

"Okay." Maddy walked over to Wyatt and hugged both him and Johnny. "See ya."

For being so young, Maddy really cared about people, and Wyatt loved her all the more for it.

The door swung shut behind Kelsey and Maddy.

"You okay, Johnny?" he asked, wondering if maybe Johnny would open up now that the others were gone.

Johnny yawned. "I wanna go to sleep now."

Frankie walked into the kitchen, and Wyatt noticed her pale cheeks were almost stark white now. "That didn't take long."

"Peter decided not to press charges but made sure Brady won't go near his daughter anymore," she whispered. "How's my little man?" she asked, leaning over to kiss Johnny's head.

"He wants to go to bed," Wyatt said and stood up, preparing to hand him off to Frankie.

Johnny tightened his arms around Wyatt's neck. "Don't leave yet, Mr. Wyatt."

"How about if I carry you upstairs?"

Johnny nodded, yawning again. "I wish you were my daddy."

Wyatt's steps faltered, and the breath backed up in his lungs. He swore his heart squeezed tight. *Me, too, bud. Me, too.*

Then he wondered if Frankie had heard what Johnny said. How would she feel about that?

Frankie led the way to her suite, then opened the door. Wyatt followed her to Johnny's room and helped her get him settled for bed.

All tucked in, Johnny suddenly grabbed Wyatt's hand. "Don't leave."

"You need to get some sleep, bud."

"Just a little while? Please, Mommy? Can't you both stay?"

Frankie looked at him, a question in her eyes.

"Sure."

Frankie took off her shoes and lay down next to Johnny, gathered him in her arms. Wyatt pried his boots off, then lay behind her and pulled them both close.

Was this what he wanted? A family? To be responsible for not just a wife, but a child…or even more children?

He'd been trying to focus on getting his life back on track, settling into the life of a rancher. Getting to know his brothers as adults, not the kids they'd been before he left.

Live down his reputation as a town rebel. Be a productive member of society.

But holding Frankie and Johnny, being there when he was needed…

It felt right.

And it scared him more than he'd ever been before.

Chapter Eleven

I wish you were my daddy kept ringing in Francine's head.

Her son's statement had shocked her the night before. And if she felt that way, how did Wyatt feel?

The words had echoed through Francine's head all night, circling and circling, until she had finally fallen asleep. At some point, Wyatt must have pulled the blanket up over them.

All three of them.

Now morning light filtered in through the open curtains of Johnny's room.

Wyatt's arm was still wrapped around her middle, his deep breaths fluttering her hair.

She raised her arm to check her watch. After seven. She really had to get ready for yet another round of meetings. The days all seemed to blend one into the other.

Their time was fast coming to an end at this idyllic ranch.

And with Wyatt.

Wyatt's arm moved, and he rubbed a hand down her hip. Nothing sexual, just comforting, and she wanted him to keep doing it.

But he sat up and rubbed his eyes. "Sorry. Guess I was more tired than I thought."

"It's fine. I'd just rather—"

"That I not be here if your father comes by, or when your coworkers start waking up."

"Sorry. But after yesterday's drama…"

He shrugged. "I get it. Family ain't easy, and neither is a family business. My pop and I butt heads about the Sullivan image, too." He stood and walked into the living room. "Watching that incident yesterday, I could see it from both sides. I was that bad boy, lusting after the prom queen, and her father threatened me to stay away from her. Hell, they all did." He cleared his throat. "Yesterday, I saw what a father goes through, wanting to protect his child."

"Yeah, I was always the good girl. I went to school, went to Dad's office more often than not, ate my vegetables and stayed far away from boys in black leather." She grinned.

"You ever regret not acting out?"

"Oh, I don't know. Maybe."

He shook his head. "If you had, you wouldn't be the amazing woman and mother you are now."

She followed him, her heart pinging at his words. "Thank you for everything you did yesterday. And for staying last night. I know it meant a lot to Johnny." She kissed his cheek. "And to me."

A muted ding sounded, and Wyatt pulled his phone out. He grimaced. "I need to get going. See you later."

She followed him to the door, watched him walk down the hallway. *What a man.* He'd been there when Johnny needed him. Had been there when *she* needed him.

Lingering at the door, she allowed herself to daydream. What would he be like as a husband? She already knew he was great with kids. She imagined herself kissing him goodbye for the day, sending him off to do ranchy stuff, while she—

While she what?

She had an MBA, had graduated from Harvard, could run a major investment company.

What could she do on a ranch in Montana?

She'd be useless outdoors, knew nothing about animals or handiwork. And indoors… She couldn't cook. Or bake. Wasn't handy with a needle and thread. She'd need something to fill her days, something with meaning.

She shook her head. She and Wyatt were a long way from having these kinds of thoughts. Time was wasting, and she was expected to open the morning meeting in forty-five minutes.

Those daydreams would have to wait for another day.

ANOTHER LONG DAY of meetings, and Francine was bone tired. Honestly, she hoped all this hard work paid off, and that the details of the merger could be hammered out before the big board meeting scheduled for November. The meeting loomed over all of them like a bomb ticking off the seconds. She just hoped it wouldn't explode in her face.

She'd been worried about leaving her son in day care all day after the events of the previous day, but Wyatt had texted her after breakfast to say he'd watch Johnny if she wanted. How had he known her thoughts? What a guy. Ready and willing to step in when she needed him. When Johnny needed him.

The man was a mystery to her. A good one, but still a mystery.

And so very good with Johnny. That was what counted the most. They had bonded almost from the first moment they met. Wyatt talked to Johnny like a person, not like a little kid.

She started to walk out of the conference room, phone in hand to text Wyatt, see where he and Johnny were.

"Francine, stay a minute, please," her father said.

She turned around, saw him still seated at the head of the table. "Yes?"

"I know it's late, and you're tired, but I'd like you to write up a report tonight. You've had several days now to assess everyone, and I want to hear your thoughts. It's critical for everyone to fold into the company, or this merger may not go through."

"Oh." She fiddled with the cuff of her blouse, disappointed. She'd hoped to spend the evening with Wyatt and her son.

"I wouldn't ask if it wasn't important."

"Can I give it to you first thing tomorrow?"

"Perfect. Thank you." He stood up and gathered papers into the briefcase. His cheeks were ruddy, which usually meant one thing.

"Are you taking your blood pressure medicine?"

"Of course," he said but didn't look up.

"Dad, you're supposed to take it every day. You can't skip any, or I'm going to call your doctor. Did you run out?"

"No. Don't worry about me. I'm healthy as a horse."

"Then why is your face that color?"

"Just tired, like everyone else."

"Why don't I order you some dinner and sit with you while you eat?"

He grimaced. "I don't need you to coddle me, Francine. I'm going to order from room service, read some reports, watch the news and turn in early."

She pointed a warning finger at him. "Promise? And no alcohol, either."

"One drink won't kill me."

"Dad, I mean it. Do I have to warn the staff not to serve you anything alcoholic?"

"You wouldn't."

"Oh, yeah? Try me." She softened, slid her arm around his shoulder. "I want you to be around a good long time, to watch Johnny grow up. Wentworth's wouldn't be the same without you."

He smiled. "You're a good daughter. Now go get my grandson out of day care and get your own dinner."

They walked out of the conference room, and he headed up the stairs to his suite just as her phone dinged with an incoming text.

She glanced at the readout to see Wyatt's text about fixing dinner for her and Johnny. Her stomach growled, and she couldn't wait to get home and see what he'd concocted. That breakfast he'd made—

Wait, *home*?

Her steps faltered. When had she started thinking of being with Wyatt as being home? She'd let herself daydream about them as a family, but those were just silly thoughts. Not real.

He's important to you. And to Johnny.

But what would happen when they left? Would they stay in touch? Or were they just like any other guests— once gone, out of mind?

She couldn't let her heart get any more involved. It would be hard enough on Johnny to leave. Maybe Wyatt would agree to at least keep in touch with her son. She didn't want him to be hurt.

Not ever again.

Chapter Twelve

Twenty-four hours later, Wyatt was still shaken by the events of the day before. Johnny had been so upset at seeing the screaming match and near fight. He'd rearranged his schedule to stay on the ranch so Johnny could spend the day with him, not wanting him to be in day care only to sneak out again.

Now he and Johnny sat on the patio in his backyard, waiting for Frankie to arrive after her meeting was finished. He would put the steaks on as soon as she got there, already had potatoes wrapped in foil and baking. Johnny had convinced him she'd want *suhmores*, too, so the ingredients were ready for later.

Johnny put his video game aside and pulled his backpack closer to him, dug inside. He pulled a book out. "Will you read to me?"

Wyatt's heart sank. "How about you read to me?"

"Don't you like reading?"

"It's okay."

Johnny handed him the book, climbed up on his lap, then opened it to the first page. "You start, and we'll take turns."

Wyatt looked at the words, at the letters squiggling around on the page. It always got worse in times of stress, which had been numerous the last couple of days. He shut his eyes, tried the calming exercises Heather had taught him. He'd gotten so much better at reading when he was by himself, but to read out loud to this little boy he loved?

And that was it.

He did love Johnny. Wished he really were his own flesh and blood.

And he didn't want to look stupid in front of the kid.

"It's okay, Mr. Wyatt. I'll start." Johnny pointed at the first word and began reading, putting his finger under each word as he went along.

How does he know?

Frankie had said he was smart. That they had tested his intelligence, and it was beyond his four years.

"Hey, guys," Frankie said, stepping out onto the patio.

"Mommy!" Johnny scooted off his lap and ran to her. She swept him up into a hug.

Wyatt stood and followed, sweeping them both into his own hug. He kissed her cheek. "How'd it go today?"

"Eh. Feels like one step forward, two steps back. But I'm sure it will get better. We're close, I know it."

"Good," he said. But at the same time, he wished it wouldn't go well. Because when they were done, Frankie and Johnny would be leaving to go back to New York.

"What have you two been doing?"

Johnny chattered on about all they had done that day, taking care of animals, fixing things.

Wyatt grabbed the steaks and put them on the grill. He opened a bottle of wine he'd gotten from the lodge, poured a glass for Frankie.

He handed the glass to her, and she smiled at him.

Just like that, his day was brighter.

"You okay eating on the patio tonight? I've got the fire pit going, and a heater in case it gets too cold. I like to stay outside as long as possible before the snow hits and we're stuck inside till spring."

"Sounds good to me." She inhaled through her nose. "It smells so good out here, between the food and the fresh Montana air."

He brought plates and utensils out to the patio and set the table.

"Can I do anything to help?" Frankie asked.

"Nope. Just relax."

"I actually have to do some work. Do you mind if I curl up out here?"

"Didn't you put in long enough hours today?"

"I know, I know. But I need to write up some notes to give Dad first thing in the morning."

"Be my guest. Let me know if you need anything."

She sat on the patio couch, and he pulled a light blanket out to cover her lap. She smiled at him, and warmth squiggled through his chest.

He went back to his dinner prep, making a salad and biscuits, talking to Johnny, answering his thousand questions about the ranch and animals. The kid had really picked up on ranch life, and he knew Johnny loved it out here.

It would devastate him and the kid both when Frankie's business here ended and they packed up to leave.

Once the steaks were done, he plated everything and called them to the table.

Frankie cut Johnny's steak for him, then sliced into hers and took a bite. He waited, hoping it was done to her liking. She sampled everything on her plate, torturing him.

She finished chewing, pointed at him with her fork. "You, sir, need to open a restaurant."

"Nah," he said, but it still pleased him that she liked his cooking. "I don't cook fancy, just plain food."

"And there are a lot of people who like that type of food."

"Too much work running a restaurant."

"But running a ranch isn't?"

He shrugged.

"I also still think you need to record professionally. That's where your true talents lie."

"Don't want to sing in public."

"Okay, but—"

"Frankie." He smiled. "Just eat, okay?"

She shrugged and went back to her food.

After dinner, she insisted on helping him with the dishes, even though he knew she was exhausted. It made for a pretty picture, the three of them in his cabin.

He shook his head. *Don't go there. She's leaving soon.*

He carried a tray of s'more items outside and set it down on the low table by the fire pit. He got Johnny's skewer readied with a marshmallow, then held one out to her.

She shook her head. "I'm still full from dinner." She leaned forward and snatched a piece of chocolate off the tray. "But I will take a piece of this," she said and bit into it.

He sat back next to her on the couch, and she pulled her tablet onto her lap, then held out a sheaf of papers to him.

"Do you mind reading this?"

"What is it? I don't know anything about investment banking."

"This isn't about that. It won't take long. Please? I need to finish my report and send it to my dad." She laid the papers on his lap. "I'm stuck on something and want to make sure I used the right terminology from this psychological study. Sometimes it helps hearing it out loud."

His shoulders hunched, dread roiling through his stomach, and he wished he hadn't eaten that second biscuit.

He looked down at the white page glaring up at him,

the words jumping all over the place. Inhaling, he tried to slow his heart rate, but it didn't help. He held the pages closer, then farther away, hoping he could focus.

She opened her mouth, but a high-pitched whine interrupted her.

Wyatt handed her the papers and jumped up.

"What's wrong? Is that Sadie?" Frankie asked.

"Yeah. Be right back." He ran inside, found Sadie lying on her bed by the fireplace. Her face was pinched, and her breathing labored.

He pulled his phone out, called Luke. "Can you come?" he asked as soon as Luke picked up. "It's time."

"Be there in five."

He hung up. "It's okay, girl. We'll get through this." He gently stroked her head and ears the way she liked.

Frankie crouched next to him. "Is she okay?"

"She's about to have her puppies."

"Oh. We should go…"

He looked up at her. "You can stay if you want. Don't know if you want Johnny to watch, but he can see them later."

She smiled at him, rubbed her hand on his shoulder. "Nervous, Grandpa?"

He tried to grin but looked at Sadie when she whined again. "Guess I am. Will you stay?"

"Sure. We'll stay out of the way. But if you need anything, let me know."

She walked back outside and murmured to Johnny.

Wyatt's nerves jangled and jumped all over the place. When he'd found Sadie wandering the fields, he'd fallen for her the minute she looked up at him with those dark brown eyes and licked his hand.

Luke walked in, doctor bag in hand. "How's she doing?"

"You're the doc. You tell me."

"She looks fine. You have everything ready for her?"

"Yeah."

Sadie yipped, and her face pinched. He rubbed her head gently, murmured to her, prayed she'd be okay and that her puppies would be healthy.

"Sing to her, Wyatt," Frankie said quietly.

He looked up, saw her standing in the open doorway, silhouetted by the light of the outdoor fire pit.

"It'll help calm her down. Maybe keep you calm, too?" She smiled at him.

Maybe she was right. Lord knew he needed to do something to keep from pacing the floor like a nervous dad in a maternity-ward waiting room.

He started singing, keeping his voice low. Sadie looked up at him and licked his hand, just as another contraction hit her.

A COUPLE HOURS LATER, Francine pulled the covers up over Johnny in Wyatt's guest room. He'd given out after the third puppy was born. Before then, he'd watched, fascinated, as each pup came into the world and Sadie cleaned them.

She walked back into the living area, shuffling in the too-big socks Wyatt had given her. He'd also lent her sweats and a flannel shirt so she didn't have to keep wearing her work clothes and could really relax.

Luke stood up from his place by the dogs. "She'll be fine tonight. Just check on them every couple of hours. I'll stop by in the morning." He glanced at Francine. "Need me to drop you and Johnny off?"

She looked at Wyatt. "No, thanks."

Luke looked at Wyatt, then back at her, raising his eyebrows. "Okay, then. See you tomorrow." He gathered up his bag and jacket and let himself out the front door.

She sank to the floor next to Wyatt, peeked into the dog bed at the four tiny blond puppies. "They're just precious."

Wyatt nodded. "It really is a miracle, isn't it?" he asked, his voice a little gruff.

Her heart turned over. This big, strong man who could heave big bundles of hay out of a truck, rope cows, fix tractors and cook like a five-star chef was still moved by the miracle of puppies being born.

He gently stroked Sadie's head and down her back. The new mother sighed and laid her head down, closing her eyes.

Francine tried to stifle a yawn but didn't succeed.

"Why don't you go to sleep? Guest room is made up."

"Are you going to sleep?"

He looked at the dogs. "I'm going to stay up a little longer."

"You're not going to bed at all, are you? You're going to be on guard duty all night, keeping watch over the puppies and Sadie."

He lowered his head, and his hair draped forward to cover his face. "Maybe," he said.

She stood up, held her hand out to him. "Come on, cowboy. Let's give Mom a little room. We can watch from the sofa."

He took her hand and stood. "You're exhausted. You should get some sleep—you don't need to stay up with me."

"I'll just keep you company for a little while."

She led him to the sofa, and they sat side by side.

He pulled a throw from the back of the sofa and covered them both with it. She snuggled up to him, and he pressed a kiss to her forehead.

"Have you ever had puppies before?"

"We've always had dogs and cats around the ranch.

But Sadie is the first of my own. I don't think I can go through this again."

He was so cute, being so worried for his dog. "It's all part of life."

"I know." He put his arm around her shoulders, pulled her closer. "You ever want more kids?"

"I haven't really thought about it. After the divorce, I threw myself even more into work. Robert burned me pretty bad—guess I've been gun-shy about getting too close to anyone."

"Haven't you dated since then?"

"I went on some first dates, mostly. But it became pretty obvious they only wanted one thing." She felt his arm tighten around her protectively. "And not what you're thinking. Those men all wanted me to get to my father. Get jobs with him, higher positions, higher salaries. A few of them found out I had a child and ran like their butts were on fire. So I finally figured it was too much bother and stopped going out."

"Jerks. Who wouldn't love Johnny? He's a great kid."

She laughed softly. "Yeah. But Johnny and me, we've been fine without them. How about you? You ever want kids?"

He was quiet for so long, she didn't think he'd answer.

"I honestly don't know. I told you I had a lot of problems in school. It was rough after my mom died. I saw what it did to Pop. I think he dated some over the years, but nothing serious. It wasn't till Kelsey brought her mother and Maddy here this summer that he fell in love. And when I say fell, I mean he fell *hard* for Bunny, from the minute they met. She's just what he needs. Hell, she's what we all needed but didn't know it till then."

He scratched his chin, and she noticed the white scar

there, almost buried by the stubble. "How'd you get the scar?" She lightly touched it.

"Uh…bar fight a few years ago."

"I hope you won."

He shrugged. "Don't really remember."

"You've had quite a life, haven't you?"

"I'm not a saint, Frankie. Never said I was."

She remembered what he'd said about being gone for a long time. "The other night you told me you'd left Montana for a while. How long were you gone?"

"Several years."

"What did you do?"

He hesitated.

"You don't have to tell me. It's none of my business."

"I had to get away from here. Away from people who knew me as nothing more than trouble. I told you I bought that old motorcycle and rebuilt it. One day I just got on my bike and headed south. Worked odd jobs at ranches. Eventually ended up in south Texas, where I lucked into a good job on a ranch. I got along with the foreman, and he taught me everything I know about ranching today."

"What made you decide to come home?"

The silence was palpable. Something had happened to him there, she just knew it.

"Ran into some…trouble…on the border, figured it was time. I'd grown up a lot by then, missed my brothers. Missed the ranch, the land. Montana is a lot different than Texas. Took a long time to figure out this is where I belong. And I had fences to mend here at home."

He still wasn't telling her everything. But maybe he'd eventually trust her enough to open up. And, she realized, maybe she'd found a man she could trust enough to open up to right back.

Till then, she'd just have to keep the startling truth she'd just realized to herself.

That she'd fallen head over heels in love with this enigmatic, brooding, caring, protective, softhearted rebel cowboy.

Chapter Thirteen

Wyatt woke with a start the next morning, his arm asleep, still wrapped around Frankie's shoulders. Adrenaline whooshed from his chest down to his legs. He hated having those damn dreams. He'd finally figured out he had them more when he was under stress or was feeling closed in.

Then he'd dream he was back in prison, with nowhere to run. He'd have to keep his back to the wall and his fists raised and ready to hit.

He'd made sure to keep his image as a badass intact for his own protection. It hadn't always worked, and he'd spent time in solitary confinement. Which he didn't mind, really. It was better than being in the infirmary after getting jumped and beaten up. He'd rather be alone, imagining he was back home in Montana rather than in a hot-as-hell Texas prison in the middle of nowhere, surrounded by desert, rocks, scorpions and orange jumpsuits.

This was the first time he'd woken up after a dream with someone, even if it was just on his couch. He and Frankie had talked for hours, and she'd kept him sane while he worried about Sadie and her puppies.

He looked down at her sleeping in his clothes. She'd come a long way from the rigid woman in the pressed pink suit and matching shoes that first day.

A lightning bolt struck him square in the heart.

He was in love with her.

Francine Wentworth. Executive vice president of a prestigious company in New York.

Wealthy, beautiful, smart, sophisticated.

Why the hell was she hanging around *him*?

Was he just a novelty, a departure from the men who used her to get to her father? A fun fling so she could break out of her mold briefly then move on to a better fit?

He didn't think that was it. At least, he hoped it wasn't.

Her phone beeped, and she stirred in his arms, then sat straight up, pushing her hair out of her face. "Oh, hi."

"Mornin'."

"Did you get any sleep?" she asked.

"Some."

"Sorry I passed out you."

He kissed her forehead. "You needed the rest."

She slid her phone out of her pocket, read the display. "I need to get going. Can I use the bathroom?"

"You don't need to ask."

She walked out, gave him a little breathing room. He wanted her so bad.

It'd been torture to have her fall asleep in his arms and not be able to take her to bed and make love to her till they both melted from exhaustion. But he wouldn't risk it with Johnny in the cabin with them. It wasn't right.

The front door opened, and he looked up to see Heather walk in. Crap. He hadn't realized it was that late.

"Heather, we need to canc—"

"Ooh! Sadie had her babies! I want to see them." She hurried over to the dog bed and crouched down. She patted Sadie's head and crooned softly over the pups.

She practically bounced over to him, and threw her arms around him. "Congratulations, Papa!"

He put his hands on her hips to push her away just as

Frankie walked in with Johnny, both of them fully dressed. The blood drained from Frankie's face, and she stopped dead.

Heather finally stepped back and saw them. "Hello!"

Frankie looked from Heather to him. "We need to go. Come on, John Allen."

"I want to see the puppies," Johnny said.

"Later. Mr. Wyatt is—" She sniffed. "Busy."

"Frankie, wait."

"You don't have to go, we're just going to study," Heather said.

Frankie stopped walking. "Yes, so I've heard." She looked pointedly at Wyatt and muttered, "Looked more like you were studying each other."

Heather, who apparently didn't hear, said, "Yeah, for the GED test."

Shit.

Frankie looked at him. "You couldn't even date someone with a high school diploma?"

A sharp pain lanced through his chest, his world collapsing all around him. The derision in her voice hurt more than all the name-calling he'd endured in school.

"Not me, silly. *He's* taking the test," Heather said. Wyatt winced as his tutor clapped her hands over her mouth. "Oops."

"What?" Frankie asked, staring at him, her eyes popped wide-open.

"Heather, could you please leave? Let's skip today," he said.

"Sure. I'm sorry, Wyatt," she said softly. "Call me to reschedule." Heather picked up her tote bag and left.

His chest ached, and it felt like he couldn't draw a full breath into his lungs. "Can we talk a minute?" He walked to the kitchen area, hoping for a little privacy.

"Sweetie, why don't you go look at the puppies? Don't touch, and be quiet, okay?"

Johnny tiptoed to the pups and knelt down to look at them.

Frankie walked up to him, her arms wrapped around her middle as if she were cold.

"I should have told you that first time you saw her."

"You mean *that's* the test you told me you're studying for? I thought it had to do with ranching stuff."

"Heather is a teacher who specializes in learning disabilities."

Her mouth opened, then snapped shut. Her face softened, and he had to look away. Didn't want to see the pity he knew would be on her face.

"Wyatt, I'm sorry for that comment. I was—" She touched his chin, turned his face back to her. "I saw you holding her—"

"For the record, I wasn't holding her. She got excited about the puppies and hugged me. I was trying to push her away when you walked in." Then her words registered. "Were you jealous? *You?*"

She nodded, her face turning red, and she looked at the floor. "I'm not proud of it."

"Frankie." He cupped her cheeks so she had to look at him. He kissed her, long and slow, poured his feelings into it, telling her with his lips how he felt.

He raised his head, watched her till she opened her eyes.

"Wow. You're a good kisser, aren't you?" she sighed.

He half smiled.

"You want to talk about it?" she asked.

He summoned his courage. "I told you I had problems in school. I was never a good student. I listened, knew the subjects, but when it came time to take tests or do classwork, I'd forget it all. When I read, it's like the letters jump all over the page and don't form words."

"That's why Johnny said you made up stories for the pictures in his book."

"Yeah. I didn't want him to think I'm stupid."

"Oh, honey. He'd never think that. He adores you. Positively worships the ground you walk on."

"You grow up with people calling you stupid and lazy, you build up defenses."

"No one knew you had a reading problem? None of your teachers? Your family?"

"Miss Bromfield—the old lady who talked to you at the diner—she spread rumors and lies about me. She was the meanest teacher, so we tended to play tricks on her to get even. But she knew it was me. Said, 'You can't fix stupid.' Everyone was afraid of her, so I guess they thought it easier to just label me a rebel, a lost cause. My family was still reeling from my mother's death back then. It wasn't till I was in pr—in Texas that I met someone who told me what my problem is. Dyslexia."

She paced away, paced back again, hands on her hips. "I want to kick that teacher's ass," she whispered so Johnny wouldn't hear.

"It was a long time ago. A small town. I didn't help myself by acting out."

"That still doesn't make it right. I want to… I want to toilet-paper her house. That mean old bat!"

He laughed, pulled her into his arms. "You would, too, wouldn't you?"

"You better believe it." She put her arms around his neck and hugged him tight.

"Well, don't do anything yet. She's the proctor for the state test in a few weeks." He pointed to the big red X on the calendar hanging on the fridge. "I don't want to piss her off just yet, or she may not let me pass. Afterward, you can do whatever you want."

She started to say something, but her phone rang. Grabbing it from her pocket, she stepped away and answered. "Yes, I'm on the way." She disconnected. "I'm sorry, I really have to go."

"Dad calling you to work?"

She rolled her eyes. "You know it." She wrapped her arms around him again. "I really am sorry for what I said. I was angry and it just slipped out, but I didn't mean it."

Pulling her close again, he wrapped his arms around her, loving the way she felt pressed against him. It felt right. He kissed her, long and hard, his lips and tongue tangling with hers till they were both breathless. "See you tonight?"

She nodded.

"The harvest festival starts in a couple days just outside town. You and Johnny want to go?"

"We'd love to. When?"

"It runs all day on Friday."

"I'm going to tell my dad we all need a break. Hopefully he'll let everyone take the day off—the team needs it after working last weekend."

"Great. I'll make dinner tonight if you want to come over."

"Sounds great. See you then."

She and Johnny left, and already he couldn't wait to see them again.

Frankie really was an amazing woman. She hadn't flinched when she found out he didn't have a high school diploma and had trouble reading. And her with a master's degree.

Maybe, just maybe, there was hope for them yet.

Chapter Fourteen

Francine had walked into the conference room twenty minutes late. Her dad had glared at her and pointedly looked at his watch. She'd sat through the proceedings, dreading the midmorning break.

She knew he'd be mad, but she couldn't very well show up in yesterday's clothing, could she?

"Take a break, everyone. Be back in twenty minutes," he said when the first break of the day came.

Bats careened in her stomach—he'd called for a longer break than usual. Extra time to lambaste her?

"Why were you late this morning?" he asked in that teeth-gritted, ticked-off voice she hated.

"I'm sorry, I just got a late start—"

"I could forgive the tardiness if you'd done the one thing I asked and gotten me your notes this morning. But you didn't."

The little girl inside her cringed, wanting to slide down the chair and under the table. The big girl inside her made her sit up straight. "I was up very late and overslept, then had to hurry back and get myself and my son ready, drop him off at day care."

"Back? Where were you that you had to hurry back?"

She opened her mouth, but his stop sign of a hand kept her quiet.

"You were with that boy, weren't you?"

Her muscles tensed, and she raised her chin. "He's not a boy, he's a man. And it's none of your business what I do in my personal time."

His eyes slitted. "It is my business when what you do in your personal time affects your time at the office. You've changed since you met him, Francine, and I don't like it. He's not a good influence on you."

"How dare you say that to me? I haven't changed. I'm still dedicated to this job and to the company."

"You've never spoken to me in that tone before. You didn't complete the report I asked for, which was important. You know I value your insight about people." His face lost that hard edge, and he suddenly looked old. "I worry about you, Francine. I always have. I want to make sure no one ever hurts you again."

She swiveled her chair around and scooted close enough to rest her hands on his forearm. "Dad, you're sweet to want to protect me."

"Of course I do. I'm your father."

She smiled. "And I love you for it. But you can't keep me wrapped in silk forever."

"I still don't think he's good enough for you," he grumbled.

"You don't think anyone would be," she teased, trying to lighten his mood.

He'd always looked youthful for his age, until today. She wanted to nag him again about taking his medicine, but all too soon the door opened and her coworkers filed in to their seats. It would have to wait until the lunch break. She didn't want him to end up in the hospital again, and this merger had really taken a toll on him.

"I'll send you the notes I have now and finish it later, okay?" she whispered.

He nodded, then opened his portfolio again.

Had she really changed since they'd arrived at the ranch? She didn't feel any different. Other than being happy for the first time in a long time. That was a good change. And Johnny had come out of his shell with Wyatt and his family. That was definitely a good thing.

Would he go back into his shell when they returned to New York?

She hoped not. For now, she had to get her mind focused on the meeting.

But doubt niggled at her, and the bats in her stomach were back.

WYATT'S PLANS FOR a quiet dinner with Frankie and Johnny were shot to hell when his dad called and said he wanted a family chuck wagon dinner that night. They hadn't done one since everyone was back home again, and it was high time.

Normally they didn't want outsiders to join them as it was true family time, but his dad allowed him to invite Frankie and Johnny.

Wyatt had gotten his chores done early that day and spent the rest of it cooking various dishes and some pies. He'd picked up Frankie and Johnny early that evening and drove his loaded truck out to the dinner spot, where Nash and his family, along with Kade and Toby, had already started setting up.

Frankie helped him set up a couple of tables while Johnny played with Maddy and Toby.

He watched the kids play. Johnny had come so far from the solemn little boy he'd been when they had arrived almost a week and a half ago. And it looked like he was having the time of his life, fitting right in with the other kids.

"Johnny loves it here," Frankie said, sliding her arm

around Wyatt's waist. "He's going to hate it when we have to leave."

Wyatt turned and pulled her other arm around his waist, sliding his own around her. "What about Frankie Wentworth, cow wrangler? Will she hate to leave?"

She looked up into his eyes. "Yes," she said, no hesitation. Then she stepped back, and he felt the loss like an ache in his chest. She unbuttoned her denim jacket, spread it open enough he could see a white T-shirt with the words Country Girl at Heart emblazoned on it with sequins.

He busted out a laugh. "Where did you get that?"

"Like it?" She did a slow turn with an extra swing of her hips. He hadn't noticed before, but she had new jeans that fit her just right, outlining her sweetheart of an ass and her long, long legs. "I did some online shopping, had these items expressed here."

He wolf whistled at her, and she giggled. "You're settling into this Montana life, aren't you?"

"It's beautiful out here. And the people are the best." She glanced around, then gave him a quick kiss when no one was looking.

Another pickup pulled up, backed in so the tailgate faced the inner circle. Hunter got out, and his boys spilled out of the front and back seats. Cody, Tripp and Eli helped unload a few things, then raced off to play with Johnny and their cousins.

"Dude," Hunter said and punched Wyatt's arm. "Frankie," he said and tipped his hat.

"Does everyone call me that now?" she asked.

"You're different than you were when y'all got here," Hunter said. "It's a good change."

Frankie looked startled, then grinned. "I think so, too." She stuck a booted foot out. "Think these would work in a Madison Avenue office?"

Hunter laughed, but Wyatt only half grinned. Yet another reminder that she'd be leaving before long. A day he was dreading with every passing moment. But honestly, why would she want to stay here? Sure, it was fine for a couple of weeks' vacation. But she was a city girl, regardless of what her shirt said.

Hunter set bags of chips on one of the tables, then wandered over to the dessert table. "All right, pie!" He turned and gave two thumbs-up to Wyatt.

Wyatt grinned. Hunter had always been a sucker for pie.

Luke arrived and parked, and right after that their dad and Bunny followed, hauling the family chuck wagon, a converted travel trailer. They used the official chuck wagon for guest dinner parties out here, but for just the family, it was easier to use the conversion.

Frankie looked around at all the pickup trucks parked in a circle. "Is this like circling the proverbial wagon train?"

"Yep," Hunter said, passing by. "You never know when the enemy might approach."

She looked at Wyatt, alarm on her face.

"He's kidding. With all the noise and the fire, no animal is going to come close," Wyatt said.

"Let's get this party started," Hunter called, and hooked up his iPhone to a speaker on one of the tables.

A country song boomed out, making the evening come alive.

Wyatt looked around at his family, laughing, talking, the kids dancing. Frankie sat on the lowered tailgate of his truck, drinking a beer, talking to Kelsey. Their heads together, Kelsey said something, and they both started laughing.

Frankie swung her legs in time to the music, and as he watched her having a good time, he began to hope they could have a future. He had a long way to go to stabilize his life a bit more. He needed to get his GED and secure that foreman job, but if he tried hard, worked at it, maybe someday he could prove himself to her. Be worthy of her.

Bunny called them to the fire for dinner. She really was good for Pop, a good addition to a family that had been all male since their mother died so long ago.

"Penny?" Hunter asked.

"Huh?"

"For your thoughts." He smiled. "What has you thinking so hard?"

"Just happy to be here."

"That's a change," Hunter said. "But a good one. Good you came home. It was about time."

Wyatt looked at his youngest brother.

Hunter shrugged. "So, I missed you."

Wyatt slung his arm around Hunter's neck, gave him a noogie. "Yeah, I guess I missed you."

"Dude, watch the hair." Hunter ran his fingers through his hair.

"You're such a prima donna." Wyatt grinned. He really had missed his brothers, even if they didn't always get along.

Nash had thrown himself into sports after their mom died, then dropped out of college and left to join the army. But he'd come home, like Wyatt had.

Kade, the good son, good dad—good in most ways, if only he could get over his ex-wife's betrayal.

Luke, who'd always brought home stray animals, even from a young age.

And Hunter. Always skating through life on his wit. Married his college girlfriend when they found out she was pregnant—with triplets, no less. Their marriage hadn't lasted long, but he adored his boys and shared custody amicably with his ex.

"Wyatt, you coming to eat?" Bunny called.

"Yes, ma'am." He shook off his thoughts, got in line for food.

FRANCINE SAT BACK in her chair at the campfire. "I don't think I can eat again for a week. Something about eating outside makes everything taste better. Thank you for inviting Johnny and me, Mr. Sullivan."

He nodded. "Call me Angus. Glad to have you with us tonight. I hope your meetings are going well."

"Going good, thanks." She didn't want to think about what would happen when the company retreat was complete. They'd be leaving.

She glanced at Wyatt sitting next to her, their shoulders brushing occasionally. Johnny wasn't the only one who would hate leaving. But she had a job to do, a merger to complete and details to finalize before the final board meeting on Monday that would make the merger official. But until then, she'd take a leaf out of Scarlett O'Hara's book and think about it tomorrow.

Bunny cleared her throat. "I've scored quite a coup. I booked a retreat for a group of romance authors after the holidays. They'll be with us for at least a week." She giggled. "And one of them is my very favorite author of all time. I'm so excited to be meeting her. She's asked to pick your brains about ranching, as she's starting a new series. I hope you'll all cooperate with her."

Francine glanced at Angus, who was smiling at his wife. She caught an odd expression on Kade's face. It looked like he wasn't happy about that particular group coming in.

Maddy popped up from her chair. "Do you like my new shickers? Daddy got them for me." She displayed one hot pink–cowboy-booted foot for Frankie, then the other, and raced off to grab a cupcake.

"Shickers?" Francine asked.

"She means shit kickers. Overheard Hunter talking about needing new ones recently," Kelsey said. "Thanks for that, by the way." She bared her teeth at Hunter.

"Hey, I can't help it if she's got bionic hearing." Hunter got up and went to his truck, then came back almost immediately with a worn guitar case.

"Hey, that's mine," Wyatt said. "Did you break into my cabin?"

"I know where the spare key is." He handed the case to Wyatt. "Play."

"Not in the mood."

"Hey, Maddy," Hunter called.

The little girl came running up to Wyatt. She clasped her hands together. "Please play, Uncle Wyatt." She tilted her head and put a pleading look on her face.

Wyatt's mouth softened into a smile for his niece as he reached for the guitar.

"You play dirty, bro," Wyatt said to Hunter.

Hunter grinned. "You better believe it." He swung Maddy up onto his lap. "She's not the only one who likes your voice. Cows and dogs like it, too."

Everyone laughed, even Wyatt, she was glad to see.

He set the guitar on his lap, and she could tell it was well used, obviously well loved, from the way he stroked it unconsciously.

She could see it keeping him company on those long, lonely nights he'd spent away from home.

He strummed several chords, then settled into a song. He closed his eyes as if to block them all out.

Up to now, she'd only heard him sing a cappella to a cow and then to his dog. But as one song blended into the next, her admiration for him grew. It was a shame he didn't want to sing in public, but she understood. This was something just for Wyatt and his family.

She looked around at his family, and everyone watched him as he sang. Even the kids had settled down around the fire.

The song he sang now was all about finding love when least expected. She saw Angus put his arm around Bunny, hold her close. Kelsey's head rested on Nash's shoulder, one hand on her pregnant belly.

Wyatt's music meant something to these people, the people closest to him.

His voice affected her, reaching deep into her soul to touch something she hadn't known she was missing, needing, just two short weeks ago.

Love.

Love for Wyatt.

Chapter Fifteen

The day after the chuck wagon dinner, Francine walked into the barn someone had pointed out to her. "Wyatt?" she called.

"Frankie?" Wyatt's voice echoed down to her.

She looked up, spotted him peering over the edge of the hayloft at her.

"Hey. What are you doing here? Is Johnny okay? Something wrong?"

He hurried over to the ladder and climbed down, fast. As soon as he touched the floor, he turned around and almost slammed in to her. "What is it?"

She stepped forward, started to hug him, but he held her arms, wouldn't let her come close. "I'm covered in dirt and hay. Been working up in the hayloft. I don't want to get your pretty clothes filthy."

"I don't care. They'll clean," she said and snuggled up to him.

"So what are you doing here?" he asked.

She leaned back so he could see her face. "It's our lunch break." She smiled. "I'm playing hooky."

"And you came to see me?"

She nodded. "I missed you. And…" She leaned closer, touched her lips lightly to his. "I didn't get a good-night kiss last night when you brought us back to the lodge."

He stared at her, each beat of her heart ramping up faster. She'd regretted not being able to properly kiss him good-night. Then she'd had some very erotic dreams about him and couldn't stand not being with him any longer.

"Then let me fix that," he said. Sliding his arms around her back, he molded her body to his so almost every bit of her was flush against him. He kissed her, once, twice, then devoured her mouth.

She met his tongue, each touch sending sparks along her spine. God, he could kiss. She could do this for days and days.

He ran his lips along her jawline to her ear, nipped her earlobe with his teeth. "I missed you last night when I went home," he rasped, his dark tone sending tingles in all the right places.

"I missed you, too."

"I wanted more than anything to have you in my bed," he whispered.

"Yeah? What for?" she asked, clutching his T-shirt, grateful to have something to hang on to when her legs grew weak.

"To explore your body, every inch of it, with my lips—" He paused, kissed her neck, her forehead, her nose. "And fingertips." He slid his hand around to cup her breast, ran his thumb over her nipple, lightly pinched it. "And—" he whispered in her ear.

She gasped, her knees really buckling this time at his words and the desperate need to have him do what he'd just said.

He kissed her again, and she tried to tell him what she wanted, how much she wanted him, with her own kisses. She lifted her leg, curling her foot around his calf, opening herself up to press against his hardness.

"Frankie, Frankie. You drive me crazy," he said, tearing his mouth from hers.

"I hope that's a good thing," she whispered.

"I can't get enough of you."

"Does the door lock?"

He raised his head, stared at her, then swept her up into his arms. He walked toward the back of the barn to a small office, and set her down just inside the door, then closed and locked it.

"You sure about this?" he asked, staring at her with those hazel eyes she loved.

She slid his T-shirt up enough to touch his heated skin, skimming her fingers over his solid abs, up his pecs, feeling the muscles that showed how hard he worked, day in and day out. Good honest work, every single day. "Touch me, Wyatt."

He slid her skirt up, his fingers blazing a trail up her thigh. It made her very glad she'd worn the longer flowing one today, and not slacks. He skimmed his fingertips over her panties.

"You're so hot," he whispered, his voice thick with desire. "For me?"

"Only you."

He groaned, his fingers clenching on her hip. It made her feel wanton, something she'd never felt before. And she wanted to explore that feeling. With him.

To think she made him feel that way? She finally understood what it was to be a sensuous woman.

She trailed her hand down his chest, down, down, down, to the front of his jeans. Pressed her hand against his hardness, felt him throb in her palm.

And swore she felt an answering throb deep inside her.

"God, Frankie. I need you. I want you so bad."

"Oh, Wyatt. I want you. Inside me. Now," she moaned in his ear, then told him just what she wanted.

He groaned again, his hand leaving her to unfasten his jeans.

She pulled her skirt up, slid out of her panties, almost desperate for him.

"Are you sure?" he asked. "You deserve more than a fast tumble in a barn."

"Wyatt, all I care about is being with you, right here, right now. I don't need fancy trappings. Just you."

WITH HER WORDS, Wyatt got lost in her. The feel of her body, her mouth on his. She was like a drug, an addiction.

He marveled that she had sought him out, in the middle of the day, in a barn, for God's sake.

But he was grateful that she didn't want hearts and flowers, fancy silk sheets or a feather bed. It wasn't his way, not at all, but she still deserved it.

No woman had ever affected him like this. Hell, there'd never been a woman like her. He wanted to touch her, all of her, body and soul.

He drowned in the feel of her wrapped around him, felt humbled when she convulsed and cried out his name, over and over.

Hell, he didn't deserve her. But for the moment, this beautiful, bright, brave woman was his, and he sent up a prayer of thanks.

She held him tight as he found his own release in her arms. This went so much deeper than just sex, deeper than two people meeting to fulfill an urge.

He eased back, saw tears on her cheeks. Panic flared. "God, did I hurt you?"

She shook her head. "Far from it. I—I just—" She took his hand, pressed a kiss to his palm.

"What is it?"

She shook her head. "Nothing."

She was so beautiful it made him ache. Dust moats floating on the sunbeams streaming through the window surrounded her, made her look like a golden-haired angel.

He wanted to tell her he loved her. But fear—fear of failure, fear of failing her, fear of failing himself, fear of his past, fear she'd reject him—kept his words bottled up deep inside him. So for now, he'd keep quiet, show her without words that he loved her and Johnny.

He vowed then and there he'd do what he could to earn the right to be with her, to love her.

And be worthy of her possibly loving him.

Chapter Sixteen

Wyatt mounted Deacon and waited for his brothers at the beginning of the gravel road. Just after Frankie left the barn that morning, they'd pretty much hog-tied him into going on a brothers' campout, like they used to do when they were young, before they'd all headed their separate ways.

He'd been hoping to see Frankie, but Nash put his foot down and said they all had to go. Long past time to do it. Besides, she'd texted him that her meeting would run really late.

Hunter reined his horse in next to Wyatt. "Did you bring pie?"

Wyatt looked at him and rolled his eyes. "Don't you ever get tired of pie? You ate most of them last night. You're gonna blow up one day."

"Tired of pie? Dude—be serious. Can't resist your pies. And if you tell anyone I said that, I'll have to kill you." He patted his stomach. "Besides, I always work off the calories." He grinned.

Wyatt shook his head. *Some things never change.* Which, when he thought about it, wasn't all bad. At least when it came to his brothers being there for each other.

When the cow patties fell, they were on hand and ready

to help. Including sending money when he needed it so he could hire a lawyer a couple of years ago.

Nash rode up, followed by Luke and Kade. "We ready to roll?"

"Where are Toby and the triplets?" Luke asked.

"Pop and Bunny are having a grandkids night, so they're up at the house," Nash said. "They even invited Johnny, since the kids all get along."

Damn. Wyatt was really tempted now to beg off so he could do some hog-tying of his own and whisk Frankie off to his cabin. Maybe he could fake a snakebite and leave the campout early.

But as he watched his brothers interact on horseback—shoving, one-upping each other with tall tales and joking around—he realized maybe he did need this time away with them. He started looking forward to sleeping under the stars that night, getting away from it all. Someday they might all go their separate ways permanently, and then where would he be?

He rolled his eyes at himself now, for the weird mood he was suddenly in, and nudged Deacon faster.

They cut off the main ranch road and angled across the meadow, galloping toward the setting sun.

"Hey, we've got an audience behind us," Hunter said, looking behind him.

They all looked back the way they'd come. Several women stood watching him and his brothers ride away from the ranch. Wyatt recognized a few of them as being on the Wentworth retreat, others as new guests. He couldn't figure out why they were all standing around like that.

"Women," Kade said, disgust evident in his voice. "They all go for romance, think cowboys and ranchers are some kind of hot commodity."

"Well, I'd say we are," Hunter said, smirking. "Imagine what they're looking at—five studly men on horse-back, riding side by side, silhouetted against the setting sun. Beautiful, just beautiful," he sniffed, pretended to wipe away a tear.

"You are such an ass," Kade said. But at least he was laughing now.

"Hey, I could write a romance book," Hunter protested.

"Just for that, you don't get any pie," Wyatt said.

"So you did bring some! Awesome."

They rode for almost an hour, to the old spot they used to camp at when they wanted to get away from their dad and his grief.

Everyone had a chore to set up camp, and they got it done fast. Wyatt had the fire going, steaks sizzling, potatoes baking in foil in no time—these being mealtime staples for him, he usually had plenty on hand. Ice-cold beer, tops popped off, and in hand, and they were ready to relax.

Wyatt inhaled, sniffing the air like a coyote scenting a hidden meal. "Man, there's nothing like the scent of a campfire and meat grilling outdoors. Someone ought to bottle it—men everywhere would buy it."

His brothers all lifted their heads and sniffed the air, and it cracked him up. "Y'all look like a pack of wild dogs."

Which of course sent Hunter off howling at the rising harvest moon.

Luke unpacked the metal plates and utensils and set them by the fire, ready for the grub.

Wyatt noticed how old the plates looked—dinged, scratched, bent in some places, definitely well used. 'Course, that was how he felt most days.

But Frankie had brought some sunshine into his life. She and Johnny both had.

Wyatt served up the steaks and potatoes on plates, handed them around, took the lid off the pot of baked beans. He didn't mind being the designated chef—at least he knew then the food would be edible.

"Hunter, how come you've had the triplets at the ranch so much lately?" Kade asked as he handed him a biscuit.

"Yvette's sick, has to get treatments a few times a week, so I get my boys to give her time to rest up." This was the first Wyatt had heard of Hunter's ex being sick. He hoped it wasn't serious. "Her parents said they'd help, but you know the boys can be a handful." Hunter's tone was light, but sounded subdued.

"Man, I'm sorry about Yvette. She's always been good to those boys," Luke said.

"Let us know if you or she need help, 'kay?" Wyatt said.

Hunter cleared his throat. "Thanks. I know she'll appreciate it."

"What do you all think about that romance author group Bunny booked for after the holidays?" Kade asked, changing the subject.

"She said at least one of them is coming to do research, right? I'd be happy to let her pick my brain—'cause you know I'm the best-looking one out of all of us, so I'm sure she'll choose me anyway," Hunter said, grinning and back to his old self.

Wyatt lobbed a biscuit at his head, but Hunter caught it in midair and took a big bite. He was always the one to try to lighten the mood.

"Some of them are probably married," Luke said. "That'd put a hitch in your plans for seduction, bro."

"Last thing we need is for the ranch to be overrun with a bunch of women, running around, poking into everything for their books," Kade said.

"Yeah, yeah. We all know you hate women," Nash said. "I admit Sheila screwed you over real good, but you—" Nash pointed his fork at Kade "—need to move on. How do you know the love of your life isn't out there somewhere, just waiting for you to find each other?"

The biscuit Kade flung hit Nash square in the head and bounced into the fire.

"Whatever. We all know you found your soul mate, Nash. Don't have to rub it in to the rest of us. Or tell us we all have that special someone out there, just waiting, pining for a big strong cowboy like me to find her," Luke said, clasping his hands against his chest and batting his eyes.

Now they all laughed, even Kade, which Wyatt thought was progress. Two laughs in one night.

"Hey, instead of picking on me, how about Wyatt? He's got someone on the line," Nash said.

"She's not *on the line*," Wyatt said, pissed his oldest brother would say that. "Frankie isn't someone to play with. Besides, she'll be leaving here soon..." His voice trailed off, and he rubbed a hand across his chest, trying to ease the ache.

"Have you asked her to stay?" Hunter asked.

"Why the hell would she want to stay out here with me? On a remote ranch? She's got a master's degree, for shit's sake. A high-powered job."

"Yeah, and a dad who'd lock her in an ivory tower if she tried to stay," Kade said. "He's kind of bossy, isn't he? I was in the conference room the other day next to where they've been meeting, and I thought he was going to throw someone through the wall. You think Dad can yell? This guy's got him beat, no contest."

Wyatt held his hands up. "Hey, no need to preach to this choir, bro."

"Yeah, I heard you've had a couple of run-ins with him," Luke said. "I wonder if Wentworth knows his golden-haired daughter helped deliver a cow."

Kade spluttered, spit his beer out. "She what?" He wiped his mouth, looked at Wyatt. "You let her do that?"

Wyatt waved him off. "Hey, I don't *let* her do anything. Woman has a mind of her own. Besides, she didn't actually help deliver it, as nimrod here says. She tried to help me keep the cow calm. And it worked."

"Her kid sure is cute," Kade said. "He latched on to you, looks up to you."

A surprising flood of emotion surged through Wyatt to realize Kade was in his corner. "Yeah, he's a great kid. As much fun as he's having here, I wonder what his life is like in New York." Wyatt cleared his throat. "I mean, Frankie's a great mom. She's just busy all the time. I'm sure the nanny gets him outside for fresh air."

"In traffic, smog and crowds?" Hunter deadpanned.

"Frankie said they go to Central Park," Wyatt said, frowning at Hunter.

"Dude, don't get defensive. We're on your side." Hunter punched his shoulder. "We all talked about it—she could be *your* soul mate."

"Why the hell would you think that?" Wyatt stared into the fire, muttered, "What would she want with a guy like me?"

"Are you kidding me? You're a catch—just like we all are. Well, 'cept Nash, who's already been caught hook, line, sinker, fry him up, that fish is *done*." Hunter cast an imaginary fishing line and reeled it in.

Wyatt had to grin. Hunter was—well, Hunter. No one else like him on the planet.

"Kade, is that movie crew still coming to film here?" Nash asked.

"Yeah. They had some preproduction delays, so now it'll be after the first of the year. They want to film in the snow anyway, make it authentic. They've got all the cabins and rooms in the lodge booked. We need to make sure the herds are cleared out of the acreage to the east."

"Dad said they're bringing trailers and vans, and I don't want the animals getting caught up in that mess," Luke said.

Kade rubbed his hand over his chin. "Let's just hope they don't blow up any of the barns."

"What barns?" Wyatt dumped the crumbs off his plate into the fire.

"Like over at the Quinn ranch," Kade said.

"What the hell happened over there? Was anyone hurt?" Wyatt asked, frowning.

"You didn't hear about it? Almost two years ago— Oh, yeah, you were…away. Shit," Kade said. "A producer contacted Mr. Quinn to use part of his ranch for filming some suspense movie. They were storing some special kind of explosives they use in movies in an empty barn, and someone accidentally blew it up. Quinn had to prove to the fire chief he hadn't done it for the insurance money. The producer forked over some big bucks to Quinn."

Wyatt tugged his hat down, stared at the orange and yellow flames. A log shifted, snapped in two, and the flames greedily attacked both halves. Two years ago he'd been locked up in a cell, desperate for someone—anyone—to believe him.

"Hey, I never did ask—did you join a chain gang? Form a love connection in the pokey?" Hunter asked, then snorted. "Ha, get it? Pokey?"

Wyatt blinked—then busted out laughing. First time he'd ever been able to laugh about that god-awful time. "You really are a shit, you know?"

"At least he's our little shit," Nash said.

"Since I'm everyone's favorite brother, can I get some pie now?"

Wyatt reached for the container holding the pies and brought out the cherry one—Hunter's favorite.

Hunter pulled a fork out of his coat pocket, held it ready and waiting. "Awesome. I call dibs on that one."

Wyatt shook his head, but pulled out the other two pies he'd made as backup and cut thick slices for everyone—except Hunter, who had dug into the cherry pie. No doubt he'd eat the whole damn thing tonight or finish it off for breakfast.

Wyatt finished his piece of pie and put the plates and the few biscuits left over into the bear-proof container. He shifted to stretch out on his bedroll next to the fire, stuck his hands in his pockets.

His brother's voices blended into the sounds of a Montana night in the valley. He stared up at the sky. The stars were so vast and beautiful—like no other place on earth.

A wolf howled somewhere, and they stopped talking, listening for how close to their campsite it might be. Another wolf answered, his howl long and undulating, one of the loneliest sounds on earth.

Wildlife notwithstanding, this was where Johnny should be growing up. This was where Frankie should want to live—endless pastureland and freedom from the pressures and expectations of her father and the company. He shook his head. What was he thinking? She had her own mind— he couldn't make it up for her.

Another log shifted in the campfire, sending a spray of sparks straight up into the air, rivaling for a place among the stars.

The temperature had dropped several more degrees, sending a cold wind over him. He buttoned up his long duster and just drifted, content to be here for the time being.

He wanted to figure out what to do about Frankie. He

loved her, and he thought she cared for him. Maybe could even love him?

Yawning, he decided he'd live in the moment and wait to see what happened.

Chapter Seventeen

Wyatt had to admire Frankie for finally convincing her
father to let them all have a day off. Wentworth had
grudgingly admitted that they were finally on track and
could take the time off as long as they spent every minute
through their final weekend working. But he'd refused to
attend the harvest festival.

Late on Friday morning, Wyatt parked his truck near
the entrance to the fairgrounds, and they all climbed out.
They got their tickets and headed inside to a whirlwind
of noise and activity. He thought Frankie's eyes were almost as big as Johnny's as they looked at everything the
festival had to offer.

Autumn flowers and leaves decorated everything from
booths to streetlights to buildings. The only thing that ri-
valed the town's decorations was the dramatic backdrop
of reds, yellows and oranges on the trees sloping up the
mountain.

He loved this time of year. The weather was crisp and
cool, but not so bad you couldn't stay outside all day. The
air smelled cold, with hints of wood burning, the scent of
coming snow and lots of fried food—the ultimate in any
festivalgoer's agenda.

He held up the schedule. "What should we do first?"

"Everything!" Johnny said.

"Okay, bud. We'll do everything." He looked at the schedule. "Mrs. Green has entries in two contests—pies and preserves. We have to be there when they announce the winners. Hey, Frankie, you might be interested in the livestock show. There are usually a lot of cows."

"Ha-ha," she said, punching his arm. "All I have to do is look out the window of the lodge to see cows." But she laughed, getting into the spirit of the festival.

He listed everything on the schedule. "And it ends tonight with an amateur talent contest and a dance."

"Well, we have to attend that," Frankie said.

"The contest?" he asked.

"No, silly. Well, we can go to that, but I meant the dance. I promise not to step on your boots...too much." She laughed.

"It's a date."

They linked hands, all three of them, and set off to explore the festival.

He usually preferred to keep to himself, didn't care for crowds, but he had to admit he was having a good time. And it was all due to Frankie and Johnny. He no longer felt quite like an outsider in his hometown.

The festival was even bigger than he remembered it being before he left. Arts and crafts booths had Frankie enthralled with handmade items, and he was loaded down with things she couldn't resist buying.

They passed one booth filled with painted canvases of all sizes. She stopped suddenly and pulled him and Johnny back to the booth.

She peered closely at the bottom of one painting. "I knew it! You've got one of this artist's paintings in your guest room, don't you? I recognized the haunting style."

He glanced at the signature. "Yep."

"Do you know the artist? Is he or she local?"

He shrugged.

She looked at each one in the booth. "All beautiful. The artist must be local—these all look like the scenery out at your ranch."

"Could be."

Turning toward him, she put her hands on her hips. "Why are you being so evasive? You know who the artist is, don't you."

He just stared at her.

"Fine. Don't tell me. I'll ask the person running the booth. These would go over big in New York."

He caught her arm just in time and pulled her close. "If I tell you, will you promise not to say anything to anyone?"

She opened her mouth.

"I mean *anyone*."

She crisscrossed an X over her heart.

"The artist paints for certain reasons but doesn't want anyone to know who he is. He donates paintings to the festival every year, and the money raised goes to whichever cause or charity needs it the most that year."

"That's wonderful. But these are gallery quality—"

"Uh-uh. You promised."

Her cheeks tinted, and she nodded. "You're right. Sorry. I'm just in love with this work. It really speaks to my soul." Her cheeks turned pink. "Does that sound silly?"

"Nope. He'd be pleased to know it. But you can't tell him. The artist is Kade," he said quietly.

She stared at him, then her eyebrows pulled together as she frowned. She glanced around quickly, then whispered, "Kade. As in your brother Kade?"

He nodded.

"Wow. I'm stunned."

"Yeah."

"Why doesn't he want anyone to know?"

"Don't know. But we all keep his secret."

"Too bad. I loved that painting in your guest room and kept meaning to ask you where you got it. Now I know."

He agreed the people who appreciated his paintings should know—Kade deserved the recognition for his talent. But he understood not wanting to be in the limelight. That's why he didn't sing in public, either.

"I want to look at these for a while. Why don't you take Johnny to play some of those games?"

"You sure? Don't mind waiting."

She glanced at her son, who was staring intently at the walkway filled with games. "I'm sure."

"Okay. Just text me when you're done and we'll meet you back here." He kissed her cheek and took Johnny's hand.

Johnny wanted to stop at every game he could play. Wyatt played a few and won several stuffed animals for Johnny, one of which was a horse bigger than the kid and seemed to be his favorite of all.

About thirty minutes later, Wyatt saw a text from Frankie that she was ready to meet them, so he and Johnny dragged all their loot back to where she waited for them.

He glanced at the booth with Kade's paintings and saw a lot of bare spots now. "Did they have a run on customers while you were in there?"

She nodded. "Hey, you two thirsty? I'd love a hot chocolate. How about you?"

"I'll get it," he said and shifted the stuffed animals in his arms to try to reach his wallet.

"You've got your hands full. I'll run over to the booth and we can sit with it during the pie-eating contest." She walked away.

"Excuse me," said a woman he didn't recognize. "You're with Miss Wentworth, aren't you?"

"Yes. Can I help you?"

"She forgot her receipt on the counter. Would you please give it to her? And tell her thanks for her generosity, and we'll get them shipped first thing Monday morning."

"How many paintings did she get?"

"Twenty! And she wouldn't take the discount for buying more than three." The woman hurried away and left Wyatt standing there, head reeling.

"Wyatt?"

He vaguely heard his name being called but didn't come out of his stupor until Frankie waved a hand in front of him.

"Something wrong?"

"You bought *twenty* of the paintings my brother did?" he whispered forcefully.

Her eyes widened. "How'd you know?"

He held up the receipt. "You left it on the counter, and the woman brought it for you. What are you going to do with twenty paintings?"

"Oh. Well, I told you I loved the work when I saw it in your cabin. I bought one for my apartment, and one for the office lobby. It'll go perfect with the decor there. The others are smaller, gifts for the team who came with us to work on the merger. I thought they could use something nice to remind them of their time out here."

"She also said you refused the discount."

"It's for a good cause. Now let's drink our cocoa before it gets cold."

She had no ties to this community, but she still wanted to support their cause. If he didn't already love her, he'd have fallen right then and there.

He looked at his watch. "Why don't you all get seats for the pie contest, and I'll take this stuff to the truck?"

"Do you need help carrying it all?" Frankie asked.

"Nope, just go on in and I'll find you in a few minutes." He gathered up their things and headed to the parking area.

On his way out of the metal gate, he bumped into someone and looked around the big stuffed horse to apologize.

Miss Bromfield.

"Excuse me, Miss Bromfield. Didn't see you—"

"*You.*" She sniffed, her snooty nose raised so high he was sure she couldn't see the ground. "You've always been a troublemaker, Mr. Sullivan."

"That's long behind me, ma'am. I'm an adult now. I don't cause problems or look for trouble. I know it's years late, but I apologize for all the pranks we played on you. I'm very sorry for any grief we caused you."

"Highly doubtful. Once a troublemaker, always a troublemaker. I'm surprised you're not in prison right now."

Adrenaline rushed through his body so fast it hurt. He clutched the various packages and toys so tight his fingers throbbed. His vision narrowed until all he could see was her mean and hateful face.

He wanted—no, needed—to walk away, get away from her spite, but his feet weren't cooperating.

She harrumphed and walked around him toward the gate.

He gulped in air, and the tight ache eased a little. "Why do you hate me so much?" he asked, but she was already gone, not bothering to answer even if she had heard him.

Laughter and excited voices surrounded him. The shrill ring from a midway game was like a drill cutting into his brain. He needed to get out of there. Be alone.

He finally forced his feet to move, and he walked fast to his truck. Dumping some of the items in the bed of his truck, he fumbled for his keys, finally got the door unlocked. He shoved everything in the back seat, then climbed in, slammed the door shut so hard the truck creaked.

A few minutes. That was all he needed. Peace and quiet.

He leaned forward, arms on the steering wheel, and rested his head.

The crushing weight of his past wouldn't let up. How could he escape it when there were reminders of it every time he came to town? The whispers and the gossip hurt more than they should. His own father didn't believe he could change. How could he expect everyone else, especially Miss Bromfield, to think any different? He should have stayed away, gone somewhere else when he left Texas.

A soft knock sounded on the passenger-side window. He looked up, saw Frankie standing there. He leaned over and opened the door.

"What's wrong? Are you sick?" she asked, climbing into the truck.

He shook his head. "Just needed a minute."

"It's been thirty minutes. I was getting worried."

"Sorry. Where's Johnny?"

"We were sitting with Kelsey and your brothers. He's with them."

"Oh."

"Did something happen?" Frankie asked.

"Run-in with my past."

She leaned her head on his shoulder, took his hand in hers. "Want to talk about it?"

"Seems like for every step forward I take, I get knocked back three."

Her hand stroked his leg, and he started to relax.

"Ran into, and I mean literally bumped into, Miss Bromfield. Let's just say her attitude toward me over the years hasn't changed at all."

"That mean old woman? Here?"

Frankie sat up, put her hand on the door handle. He grabbed her arm before she could open it.

"What? I'm just going to go kick her ass," she said.

He pulled her back against him. "Why?"

"Why what? Why do I want to hurt her? Because she hurt you."

"Why do you keep hanging around me? Jumping to my defense?"

She turned toward him, ran her fingers through his hair, brushed it off his cheeks. "I—I care about you, Wyatt."

Closing the distance, she kissed him. But he couldn't help wondering if there was something else she was going to say.

The one thing he wanted to say but was too scared to tell her.

Chapter Eighteen

It had taken Francine some convincing to get Wyatt back to the festival. She and Johnny did their best to put him in a better mood, but hurt still lurked behind his eyes, and the few times he did smile, it was only a half-hearted attempt.

As the sun set, they ate dinner with Wyatt's brothers and their families, then trooped to the open-air pavilion for dancing under the stars.

A special tent had been set up for the kids to do arts and crafts and play board games while the grown-ups danced. When Maddy and her cousins all begged to go there, Johnny said he wanted to as well, which shocked her. He'd blossomed so much the last couple of weeks.

She and Wyatt checked him in with the woman in charge of the kids' tent.

Francine knelt in front of him. "Now promise me you'll stay close to Maddy and her cousins, okay? If you want to be with me and Wyatt, you tell this nice lady here, and she'll call me."

"Yes, Mommy."

"Have fun tonight, sweetie."

"You, too, Mommy! 'Bye!" He raced over to the table where the Sullivan kids sat.

"I don't think he'll miss me at all tonight," she said, and stood up.

"Doesn't look like it. Guess that means you can have some fun, huh?" Wyatt grinned at her and winked.

They left the tent and Wyatt took her hand, linking his fingers with hers as they walked to the dance floor. It sent shock waves up her arm, across her shoulders and down to her heart. How could something as simple as holding hands mean so much?

But it did, and she savored his touch. His fingers were strong and sturdy, his palms callused. Occasionally his thumb would stroke her hand, and she tingled in so many places.

He led her to the dance floor and turned to face her. Unlike the first time they danced at the barbecue, she willingly went into his arms. Two uncoordinated feet or not, she meant to savor every minute of tonight.

The band started another song, a slow one, and he pulled her closer, their bodies melding as one in time with the song. She laid her head on his shoulder, closed her eyes, and his arms tightened around her. It was more like hugging to music, and she loved it. Didn't want it to end, wanted to stay that way forever.

She opened her eyes and stared at his neck. Moving her head just a touch, she was able to kiss his neck. She nudged his hair back and gently bit the skin just above his jacket collar.

Wyatt jerked, his hand flexing on her hip. "What are you doing?"

"I've never given anyone a hickey before." She raised her head and grinned at him.

"You keep doing that and I won't be held responsible for what happens next."

"What? You'll give me one back?"

His eyes mesmerized her as he studied her face. "Yup. But not where anyone can see it." He lowered his head and spoke into her ear. "It'd be a secret, just between you and me. And every time you'd see my mark on your smooth skin, you'd remember the feel of my mouth on your body."

She gulped, and her body went flaming hot. Taking a step back, she stared at him, then grabbed his hand and tugged him off the dance floor.

She wanted him now with a desperation she'd never felt before. Looking all around, she tried to find somewhere private they could go.

"What are you looking for?" he asked, his voice husky.

"Someplace we can be alone," she said, frustrated.

His eyes squinted, and he looked up toward the sky. "I know a place."

"We can't leave. I just want a few minutes alone with you. Now."

"Not leaving. Come with me."

This time he pulled her through the crowds toward a row of buildings on a side street just outside the festival tents. He walked past the first building on the corner and ducked into an alley, taking her with him.

He stopped at a door cloaked in shadow. "Earlier I saw this building is still vacant. Wanna be a rebel tonight, Frankie?"

She nodded, not able to speak.

"Keep an eye on the street, make sure no one sees us." He faced the door and she heard a soft bang, then metal grating on metal.

She glanced at him and saw the door stood open now. A light flashed—he'd pulled his phone out to light the way.

"Did you just break in?" A little frisson of fear interrupted her excitement.

"Nope. Well, not really. I just know the trick to opening the door. Call it a talent I picked up in my youth."

"I don't know about this. Is it safe?"

"I wouldn't bring you here if it wasn't. I thought you wanted a little rebellion tonight."

She hesitated.

"Come on, little rebel." He held a hand out to her, and she took it. He led the way to a staircase, his phone lighting the path in the deserted building.

Nerves and excitement warred together, coupled with an intense desire for this man.

She'd never done anything like this, even as a teenager. She hadn't been kidding when she'd told him she'd never acted out, had always been a good girl.

Tonight that would all change. Her own little rebellion with Wyatt. Tingles danced across her back and down her spine, and she experienced something she never had before. The need to be a little naughty.

The stairs ended at a door. Would her adventure end now?

He tapped the door just above the knob, then turned it. The door opened, and she realized they were on the roof. He led her outside into the cold air.

They walked to the parapet bordering the edge of the roof. It was just low enough for her to lean on and look over.

"Oh, we're right over the festival!" She looked all around at the bright lights on the dance floor, the flags waving in the breeze, then up at the zillions of stars in the sky. Even with the limited lights from the town, she could easily see them all.

Warmth covered her back as Wyatt stood behind her, pressing his body to hers. "What was that about being a hickey virgin?" he asked, his voice low.

She turned around in his arms so she faced him. "I've never gotten nor given one," she said, surprised at the huskiness in her voice. "You want one?"

He nodded.

"Where?"

He opened his denim jacket, unbuttoned his flannel shirt. "Right here." He pointed to his left pec. "So I can see it if I look down, or in the mirror. And think of you," he said.

She licked her lips, staring at his chest. Leaning forward, she kissed the area he'd pointed to, then licked it, heard his sharp intake of breath. She bit lightly, sucked the skin between her teeth, soothing it with her tongue.

His hand gripped her hips, and he pressed against her. He was so hard she gasped. Heat pooled low in her belly, and she scraped her nails lightly across his chest.

She pulled back, saw a dark mark on his pec, and it excited her to know she'd put her own mark on him. But it didn't compare to the mark he'd left on her soul.

Slipping her hands between them, she unbuttoned her blouse, watched him watching her. The cold air hit her chest, and her nipples tightened even more than they had been.

He slipped his arms around her, arching her back, pulling her upper body closer. Bending over, he latched on to her breast through the lace of her bra.

She let her head fall back and just let herself feel. Tonight was all about reveling in Wyatt, even if they were stealing just a short time away together.

His lips and tongue traced her skin along her bra line, then he bit down gently, in the same spot she'd marked him. Happiness filled her that he wanted their marks to match.

She raised her arms and caressed his head as he gave her pleasure. Running her fingers through his hair, she savored the silkiness.

He lifted his head and looked at her chest. She looked down, saw the love bite he'd given her. She traced the mark with her index finger, dipping down just beneath the edge of her bra.

He groaned.

And she smiled.

He kissed her, and the power behind it, the intensity, took her by surprise. Their tongues tangled, and every stroke of his sent her higher, made her crave more. She pressed her hips to his, frustrated by the amount of clothes between them.

But they were on a roof in the middle of town. What could happen? They couldn't even go out to his truck in case people walked by.

"Turn around," he said.

"Why?"

"Just do it," he rasped.

She complied, felt him lean against her again. He took her arms and laid them out along the parapet. "Keep your arms there."

"What are you doing?"

"Tonight's about your pleasure."

Cold air slid across her legs as he raised the back of her denim skirt, and goose bumps prickled her skin. His hands glided down her legs, taking her panties off.

She heard the rasp of his zipper, then his hands were everywhere at once. He caressed her bottom, her stomach, her breasts. She couldn't keep up with the sensations and finally let them spill over her, one after the other.

He slid into her, filling her body, filling her heart, filling her soul.

No one had ever touched her this way. Honestly, if she could finally admit it to herself, no one had ever made her feel this way, taking her to new heights with every stroke, every touch.

"You're so beautiful, Frankie," he whispered against her hair. "I've never met anyone like you before."

His words set her free, and she came hard and fast, clenching her hands on the brick parapet. He followed her, grating out her name, over and over.

He moved back, and she mourned the warmth of his body.

She turned around and shook her skirt down, put her panties back on. She couldn't believe what she had just done. Peeking over the edge of the parapet, she didn't see anyone pointing up at them.

"Shit," Wyatt said.

"What's wrong?" She turned around to see him calling someone.

"A 911 text from my dad."

Fear clutched her heart that something had happened to her father.

"Pop, what's wrong?" Wyatt asked. His whole body tensed. "We'll be there in a few minutes." He hung up and grabbed her hand. "We need to go."

"What is it? What happened?"

"A security guard found Johnny sleeping in one of the empty tents. He's at the police station. A deputy recognized him from the other day, called my dad when they couldn't reach you."

She grabbed her phone out of her pocket, saw it was dead. "I knew I shouldn't have let John Allen stay at the kids' tent." She ran to the door and hurried down the stairs, feeling her way in the dark.

"Frankie, wait for me. I've got the light." He caught up to her at the bottom of the stairs, shone the light as they left the building.

"Where's the police station?"

"About a mile from here. Come on." He grabbed her

hand, but she pulled away, saw the hurt flash across his face. She started running to the parking lot. She'd have to apologize later. Right now she had to get to her son. He'd been alone and scared, and she'd been off having fun.

Anything could've happened to him. And if something had, she'd never forgive herself for letting her guard down.

WYATT PULLED UP to the police station and parked in front. He stared out at the sign lit up like a glowing neon reminder of his past.

Frankie shoved the passenger door open. "Are you coming or not?" All he could do was stare at her, his voice frozen.

She got out and ran to the front door but looked back at him, then yanked the door open and disappeared into the building.

This was his fault. He'd convinced Frankie to have a little revolt against her respectable life. To live on the wild side, even if it was no more than a half hour on the roof of an abandoned building. With him.

He'd come home to change his life, to live quietly and stay out of trouble. Now he'd brought it to the woman and child he loved more than anything.

Forcing himself to shove the heavy door open, he finally got out of the truck. Each step up the sidewalk to the door felt like he was sinking in quicksand, or mired in thick, black tar. Reaching out to open the grimy glass door, his hand shook. He made a fist, inhaled a deep breath, then bit the bullet and opened the door.

Walking into the station, the chemical smell of industrial cleaners assaulted him, and he flashed back two years ago. Adrenaline spiked so high it made his head hurt.

The police radio squawked an emergency call, echoing

around the room. Sweat trickled down his back, making his shirt stick to his clammy skin.

Two men across the lobby caught his attention—Pop and Mr. Wentworth.

Wyatt pushed himself across the lobby, his boots scuffing the cracked linoleum. "How'd you beat me here?"

"We were in town having dinner when the sheriff called because they couldn't reach Francine," Pop said.

An electronic door in the back of the station buzzed open and a deputy escorted Johnny out.

Johnny saw Frankie and ran to her. "Mommy!"

She fell to her knees and grabbed him in a hug.

Wyatt moved to go to them, but his dad stopped him.

Wentworth hurried over to her and Johnny. "Come on, Francine. Stand up." He helped her up, patted Johnny's back.

Wyatt shook his dad's hand off and moved to Frankie and Johnny. "You okay, bud?"

Johnny nodded but didn't reach out to him, which cut him in half.

"They don't deserve to breathe the same air as you," Wentworth said to Wyatt.

"Stop! Don't talk about him like that," Frankie said.

"I had him investigated, Francine."

"Y-you what?" Wyatt asked, fear making him feel like he'd puke.

"Did you know he'd been in prison?"

She nodded. "Yes, he told me. In high school. He was innocent."

"No, he was arrested a couple of years ago for smuggling drugs across the Mexican border into Texas, and he went to prison. He's an ex-con, Francine. You shouldn't be around someone like him. Nor should my grandson."

Wyatt's world caved in, and he didn't know which

way was up. Breath backed up in his lungs. He looked at Frankie, wanting to beg her to understand.

But she stared at him like she'd never seen him before. Worse, like he was the criminal her father accused him of being.

"It's not true—" he said, reaching for her.

She jerked away from him, and it was like she'd stabbed him in the heart. "Why didn't you tell me before? You had plenty of opportunity."

"I was ashamed—"

"I need to get my daughter and grandson to the ranch. It's been a long day, and I don't want this to continue."

"Take my car," Pop said and handed his keys to Wentworth.

Wentworth pulled Frankie and Johnny close, led them past him and out of the station.

He started to follow them, but his dad stopped him. "Let them go."

"I need to explain to her, tell her what really happened."

"Tomorrow, son. Emotions are too high right now. Come on. Let's go home."

Wyatt handed his keys to his dad, afraid he'd crash his truck trying to get them back to the ranch.

Nothing had ever hurt this much. He just prayed she'd listen to him in the morning.

And not that he expected Pop to come to his rescue, but he'd just stood there, not saying a word, when he knew it wasn't true. It cut him deep—his own father.

Chapter Nineteen

Wyatt had spent a sleepless night thinking about nothing but Frankie and Johnny. One minute he prayed she'd believe him and stay, the next he knew he wasn't the right man for her.

He barely waited for the sun to come up before he high-tailed it to the lodge. He drove up and parked in front, noticed a sleek black limousine being loaded with luggage. Hurrying up the steps and inside, he took the stairs two at a time up to Frankie's room.

He knocked on the door, hoping, praying she'd answer and not slam it in his face.

Wentworth opened the door. "What do you want?"

"I need to see Frankie."

"Her name is Francine. She doesn't want to see you."

"Please, sir. I need to explain."

Wentworth stepped outside and closed the door. "You need to go. We're leaving right now."

"I need to see her—"

"Don't you get it yet? You're not the right man for her and John Allen. While you were jailed for pranks in high school before going to *prison*, my daughter was making something of herself, working hard for my company and to be a good mother to John Allen. And last night, while you two were off exploring, my grandson went missing and no one knew it."

As much as the words hurt, he knew Wentworth was speaking the truth. He wasn't the right man for Frankie, even if he loved her beyond words.

"Can I say goodbye to her and Johnny?"

"Make it brief," Wentworth said and opened the door.

Wyatt walked into the suite just as Frankie came out of the bedroom. "How's Johnny?"

"He's fine."

"How are you?" He hated the shadows beneath her eyes, hated that he'd put them there.

"I'll never forgive myself for going off last night."

"It wasn't your fault—"

"I wasn't finished," she said, cutting him off. "Why didn't you tell me about being an ex-con? You told me about living in Texas, working on a ranch, but you conveniently left that part out."

"I know. I wanted to tell you, but I didn't want you to look at me the way you did last night."

He moved closer to her, but she stepped away.

"Did your dad tell you about the rest of the report?"

She frowned, shook her head.

"I was innocent. I'd gone to Mexico with someone I thought was my friend. Coming back, he saw they had the drug-sniffing dogs out, so he put the drugs he'd bought in the bag on my bike when I wasn't looking."

He walked away, rubbing a hand across his face. "I spent five long, hard months in a Texas prison until that same friend was arrested and he confessed to what he'd done. It took time to get things straightened out, but they finally cleared me of any wrongdoing and let me go."

"So you really were innocent," she said, touching his arm. "I'm sorry, Wyatt. Sorry you had to go through that, and for last night, thinking you'd lied to me. Once burned and all that. My ex has made me sensitive to lies."

She wrapped her arms around his neck, hugged him tight. Relief washed through him that she believed him. But he had to make the break.

He pulled her arms down, had to push himself away from her for the next part. "Your dad said you're all leaving this morning. That's a good thing."

"I'm heading back earlier than expected, but it's only to prepare for the board meeting. Once we complete the merger… I thought Johnny and I would come back and we can explore what we have between us."

"Frankie—Francine," he started.

The smile left her face, inch by inch, until she looked made of marble.

"I'm not the right man for you, or for Johnny. I don't want to hurt you—either of you—but this is for the best. I need to concentrate on getting past this, get my diploma."

Her lips trembled, and she pressed her fingers against them. "You don't want to hurt me? What do you think you're doing right now?"

"You deserve so much more than what I can give you."

"You mean love? Because I love you, Wyatt. Johnny and I both do. We need you—"

Her words made him double over, grief coursing through his entire being. He forced himself to stand up, step back. "I can't." Flustered, he sought for the words to explain. "You're a high-powered executive. I can barely read."

"But that doesn't matter—"

"Maybe I don't love you," he lied. "I could never give you what you deserve. I don't want to cause you any more trouble, either one of you." He walked to the door and looked back once. He wished he hadn't, because now he could see firsthand what he was feeling. Because it was written all over her face.

He opened the door and walked out. Wentworth stood by the stairs.

"I told her." Wyatt stepped close to Wentworth, meeting the man's eyes. "Promise me you'll take care of her and Johnny."

Wentworth nodded.

"I mean it—you promise me she'll be okay, that she'll be happy." His voice cracked, and he blinked back tears.

Wentworth's face paled and he stepped back, stared at him. "I'll make sure she's fine. She and my grandson."

Wyatt turned and walked down the stairs.

Leaving the lodge, he walked to his truck, then saw the stuffed animals he and Johnny had won, and Frankie's packages. He couldn't look at them ever again, so he grabbed an armload and took them to the driver loading the limo.

He'd just brought the second load to the limo when Wentworth walked outside. Frankie followed, holding Johnny's hand.

"Mr. Wyatt!" Johnny broke free, hurled himself at Wyatt.

He bent over and caught Johnny, knelt down and wrapped his arms around the son of his heart.

"I don't wanna leave you!" Johnny cried, his little body shaking with sobs. "I want you to be my daddy."

Wyatt's heart broke even more, Johnny's tears killing him. "I love you, bud. I always will. Don't forget that, ever," he said, fighting his own tears. "I'd love for you to be my son," he said, his voice breaking.

Johnny's arms squeezed tighter around Wyatt's neck, holding on like he'd never let go.

And Wyatt didn't want to let him go—to let either of

them go. But he had to, for their sake. He pulled Johnny's arms down. "But you need to go now."

"John Allen, come here," Wentworth demanded.

"Go on, Johnny. Go to your granddad."

"No," Johnny cried, his voice muffled in Wyatt's shoulder.

Wyatt picked him up, took a step closer to Frankie, her face a stone mask, her arms wrapped around her middle.

She leaned forward and took Johnny from Wyatt, then moved away quickly.

"No!" Johnny screamed. "I want Mr. Wyatt!" he cried, tears pouring down his face.

Wentworth got in the limo, leaving the door open. Frankie climbed in, holding tight to her sobbing son.

When the door closed, Wyatt watched the limo drive by him. Frankie looked out at him once through the open window, tears running down her cheeks.

All he could do was stand there, broken and devastated, watching his life drive away from him.

Chapter Twenty

Wyatt threw the hammer across the equipment barn and it crashed into the old red tractor, clanging like an alarm bell.

The tractor he and Johnny had fixed.

He'd never experienced a longing like this, so acute it was a physical pain. He rubbed a hand across his chest, trying to ease the tight, persistent ache.

He missed Johnny's bright chatter, his interest in everything on the ranch. He missed Frankie's laughter, and the way she felt in his arms.

Nothing helped.

Not booze.

Not his guitar.

Not even riding his bike—any time he got on it, he felt the ghost of Frankie hugging him tight from behind, squeezing the breath out of him.

He couldn't sleep, couldn't eat, he barely functioned. His eyes burned, and he pinched them closed against the sting.

He'd been pushing himself for two weeks—since Frankie and Johnny walked out of his life.

Correction—since he'd shoved them out.

The door opened, and his dad walked in. "There you are. Need to talk to you a minute."

Great. What'd he do now?

"I've thought long and hard about this, and I want you to be the new foreman. You've proven to me you can do the work, that you aren't going to take off and abandon us again."

"I didn't abandon y'all," Wyatt snapped.

"It felt like you did. You and Nash both gone—I'd lost both of you, and it hurt."

Wyatt stared at his dad, having trouble understanding what he meant. "I didn't think you wanted me around. We never got along."

Pop looked down, then back up. "It's taken me a lot of years—and poking and prodding from Bunny—to realize I took your mother's death out on you boys. I never stopped loving any of you, but her death nearly killed me. And I retreated from everyone. I can never apologize enough."

For the first time in his life, Wyatt understood now what his dad had gone through after her death. Because losing Frankie and Johnny had been like a death.

He closed the distance and grabbed his dad in a hug. "I'm sorry, Pop. Sorry Mom died, sorry for leaving, sorry for not being a better son."

Pop hugged him back, hard, clapped him on the back.

Wyatt stepped away, and his dad wiped his eyes.

"So anyway, do you want the job?"

"Yeah. Thank you. I won't let you down, Pop."

"See that you don't." He cleared his throat. "I'm sorry about Francine. I know it hit you hard. But it will get easier, truly it will."

"I had to let her go. It'll never get easier."

His dad opened his mouth, but Wyatt held a hand up. "It's okay, Pop. I'm not ready to talk about it just yet."

Pop nodded his head, and with a final clap on his son's shoulder, walked out of the barn.

Wyatt strode across the empty space to the worktable,

kicked a box out of his way. Well, at least he'd gotten the job he'd wanted.

He paced back to the other side of the barn, kicking the same box out of his way yet again.

"Did you kill it?" Hunter asked behind him.

Wyatt looked behind him as Hunter and the rest of his brothers filed into the barn. "Kill what?"

"That box. I don't know what it did to you, but I hope it learned its lesson."

"Don't be an idiot," Wyatt said. "What do y'all want?"

"We all," Hunter began, and waved a finger to indicate their other three brothers, "think you're the idiot."

In a flash, Wyatt was back in the schoolyard, kids taunting him, calling him stupid. But this time it hurt even worse considering it was his own brothers thinking he was stupid.

"You're an idiot for letting Frankie leave," Nash said.

"You mean like when you let Kelsey leave?" Wyatt snapped back.

"I didn't *let* her leave. She ran. And I tried like hell to find her."

Hunter held an envelope out to Wyatt.

"What is that?"

"Open it," Nash said.

Wyatt opened the envelope and pulled out an airline ticket.

He squinted, concentrated on the words. A ticket to New York City.

He held it up. "What's this for?"

"Go get her," Hunter said.

He frowned, jerked his head. "I can't. I'm not the right man for her."

"Do you love her?" Nash asked.

Wyatt looked at Nash. "Yes."

"Would you die for her?"

"It feels like I already have," he said quietly. "But with my past—"

"That right there is the key word—*past*. What happened, happened. Have we all made mistakes we regret? Yes. But you can't undo it, can't relive it. Just move forward. What matters is that you love her, will take care of her and Johnny, and do your best by them, right?" Nash pointed at him.

"But her dad agrees I'm not right for her. He'll never accept me and that'll weigh on Frankie and Johnny. I can't—"

"No father ever thinks any man is right for his daughter. You think Maddy will have it easy when she starts dating? Won't happen till she's forty, but she's got me, four uncles and four male cousins—five if you hurry up and go get Frankie."

Wyatt grinned, getting his point. He waved the ticket. "But I don't even know where she lives. New York is a huge city."

Hunter held out another piece of paper.

Wyatt eyed it like it was flaming bull cookie. "What's that?"

"You may not know where she lives, but you do know where she works. Wentworth & Associates, Fortune 500 company. It's in the phone book. On the internet." Hunter tapped the piece of paper. "And the address is on this piece of paper."

"Your flight leaves tonight at eight," Luke said. "Couple of stops, but it's the fastest way to get you there."

Wyatt glanced at Kade. "What do you think?"

Kade grimaced. "Women are evil creatures, designed to torment men."

"That was just your ex-wife. Not every woman is like Sheila," Hunter said.

"Whatever. As I was saying, women are made to torture men. But you're miserable without Frankie and Johnny, you're snapping and snarling at all the ranch hands—and all of us—so I agree. Go get them." Kade help up a slim jeweler's box. "And you can give her this. Housekeeping found the necklace on the floor behind a chair in her suite."

Emotions crowded in Wyatt's chest, battling to take hold.

"I'll take Sadie and the pups to my place and take care of them," Luke said.

"Thanks, guys. All of you. I mean it," he said, his throat tight. Before he broke down, he ran out of the barn, got in his truck and sped to his cabin.

He prayed he could apologize enough to Frankie, and that she'd understand why he'd hurt her and Johnny.

Hope blossomed in his chest, and that tight ache eased a bit.

The three of them.

A family.

Chapter Twenty-One

Wyatt was grateful to his brothers for booting his ass out of Montana to get Frankie. He'd gotten off the plane and into the swirling madness of a New York City airport, grabbed a cab and was now stepping out into a tidal wave of people. He fought his way through to the revolving door of Frankie's office building and walked into quiet.

He really hoped she hadn't taken a long weekend or was in meetings out of the office.

He walked toward the security guard's desk, and an older black man stood up.

"Help you, sir?" the guard asked.

"I'm here to see someone on the—" he checked the paper Hunter had scribbled on "—forty-second floor."

"Do you have an appointment?" the guard asked, reaching for a clipboard.

"An appointment?" *Great.* "No. It was a spur-of-the-moment trip. Do I need one?"

"Yes, sir. Who are you here to meet with?"

Wyatt shook his head, feeling lower than a flea on a tick. "All the people who work here, I'm sure you don't know her."

"I can ring upstairs for you."

Wyatt grimaced. "I was hoping to surprise her."

"Who?"

"Like I said, I doubt you know her. Francine Wen—"

The guard smiled for real this time. "Ms. Wentworth. Charming lady. Just returned from Montana…" His words trailed off, then his eyebrows popped up. "From a ranch in Montana," he said, looking at the hat on Wyatt's head.

"That's my ranch—well, I'm part owner. She told you about it?"

"Ms. Wentworth always stops by to ask about my grandkids. She mentioned it when she returned a couple weeks ago." The guard leaned forward and lowered his voice. "She's one of the very few who take time to do that." He leaned back again.

Wyatt grinned, the first time it felt genuine in who knew how long. "That's my Frankie…er, Francine."

The guard reached for something on his desk, handed him a slim black key card. "Seeing how you and Ms. Wentworth are old friends, I'll let you go on up and surprise her. Just sign in here, then use this key card in the elevator. Be sure you bring it back to me. My name's Oscar."

"Thanks, Oscar. I sure appreciate it."

Wyatt headed to the elevators and was soon whisking up to the forty-second floor in a sleek, modern chrome-and-glass cube with some kind of classical music piped in. Might have been elegant and classy, but he still felt trapped, closed in.

He knew for a fact he'd never been in a building this tall.

And he never wanted to do it again.

The minute he'd landed, he'd felt everything closing in on him—people, buildings, cars. He wanted to get Frankie and Johnny and head home, to the boundless countryside, where the wildlife outnumbered the people. Like it should be.

Here there was wildlife of a different kind. And he didn't like it one bit.

The elevator opened into a quiet lobby with paneled walls and modern artwork. He stepped out onto carpet so thick his boots sank into it. Every stick of furniture was so polished he could see reflections. Glass gleamed and sparkled everywhere, and it all looked like money. Lots and lots of money.

"May I help you, sir?" an equally polished woman asked as he approached the large desk in the middle. Wentworth & Associates was emblazoned on the wall behind her in gold lettering.

"I'm here to see Francine Wentworth, please."

"I believe she's in a meeting, but let me buzz her assistant." The woman punched a button, then spoke quietly into her headset, then glanced up at him. "Ms. Wentworth's assistant will be with you shortly. Just have a seat over there."

Wyatt walked toward the chairs and couch in front of the windows. The wall opposite the windows was gleaming, polished wood—and held one of Kade's paintings. It was one of the biggest pieces he'd done during a particularly rough time. A muted winter scene, all gray and white, with the barest hints of the colors of sunset. Frankie was right—it fit in great with the furniture.

"I'm Isabella, Ms. Wentworth's assistant. How may I help you?"

"Wyatt Sullivan, ma'am," he said, turning to another polished woman with hair slicked back into a tight bun. "I need to speak with Frankie—Francine for a minute, please."

"What is this in reference to?"

"It's personal."

"And how do you know Ms. Wentworth?"

"Your executives stayed at my ranch for two weeks. As I'm sure you know, if you're a good assistant."

Her eyebrow quirked up ever so slightly. "Yes, sir. What do you need to speak with her about? Maybe I can help you?"

He shook his head. "Sorry, it's personal."

"Ms. Wentworth is in a very important meeting and cannot be disturbed."

He waved his hat toward the chairs by the window. "I can wait over there till she's done."

"I'm afraid the meeting will last the rest of the day. You wouldn't be very comfortable here," she said, raking her eyes from his messy hair to his dusty boots.

"Look, ma'am, I've just traveled seventeen hours from Montana to speak with Ms. Wentworth in person. I promise it won't take long. I just need to ask her one question."

She pursed her ruby-slick lips. "I repeat, I'm very sorry, but she cannot be disturbed. If you'd like to leave a note or your number, I'll give it to her when she's free tonight."

"Fine."

She handed him a small notebook covered in leather as soft as…well, as soft as the hide of a newborn calf.

He paced away from her for some privacy and scribbled a note, tore it out of the notebook, handed it back to her. Isabella took the notebook back, then pulled an envelope out of the back of it.

The note went in the envelope, and he dug the jewelry box out of his pocket, tucked it inside with a prayer Frankie would be receptive. He handed it over to Isabella, then turned and walked to the elevator. He punched the button and glanced back to see her watching him. *Making sure me and my dusty boots leave, I'm sure.*

The elevator whisked him back to the ground floor as silently as it had taken him up. He exited, then walked back to the guard station.

Oscar stood up, smiled at him. "Did you see Ms. Went-worth?"

Wyatt shook his head. "Her dragon wouldn't interrupt a meeting," he said, handing the key card back to the guard.

Oscar laughed. "Yes, that's definitely Isabella. I'm sorry you didn't get to see her. Will you be in town for a while?"

Wyatt pointed with his hat out the door. "I left her a note that I'll be waiting down here in that little coffee shop, if that's okay."

"Very good, sir."

Wyatt walked into the café, bought a bottle of water and a muffin, then settled in to wait.

HOURS PASSED. The sunset came and went, and Wyatt could barely keep his eyes open. He'd given in and bought a newspaper earlier, and slowly worked his way through all the news about a city he couldn't wait to get the hell out of. Oscar had finished his shift, stopped by to wish him luck.

He checked his watch—well after eight o'clock, and the coffee shop server had said they would be closing soon. He stood up to stretch and glanced around the lobby for the fifteen hundredth time.

And saw her.

His Frankie.

At least he thought it was his Frankie. Except tonight she was definitely Francine Wentworth. She was dressed real fancy in some sort of expensive navy blue evening dress and a fur coat, for Pete's sake. Her hair was pulled up fancy-like, and the diamond earrings dripping from her earlobes were so big he could see them sparkling all the way across the lobby.

Her father stepped up next to her and they walked out of the building just as a sleek black car stopped in front of them. The driver hurried around to open the door and then whisked them away.

And she never looked his way.

Not once.

I guess I have my answer.

Chapter Twenty-Two

Monday dawned gray and chilly, and a brisk wind blew Francine into the office building. The dreary weather matched her mood perfectly.

She still hadn't forgiven her father for not telling her the true story about Wyatt's imprisonment. Upon her return to New York, she'd had to demand his assistant give the private investigator's report to her. Reading it had broken her heart.

She hated the thought of him cooped up in a metal cell for so long. Alone, no family or friends. No one on his side. No wonder he'd gone back to Montana, with the wide-open spaces. She'd had several nightmares about him being in prison, and her heart ached for him.

But he'd pushed her away, said he wasn't right for her. He might have been innocent, but it had to have been a terrible thing to admit to going through. It still stung that he hadn't trusted her to tell her the truth earlier. They'd have worked through their differences by now and could already be planning a life together.

It had been a rough two weeks—Johnny was still despondent about leaving the ranch. She'd really thought he'd be dealing with it better by now—but then, she wasn't, either. Every time he cried, she nearly broke down.

She'd never really watched television much, but now she

kept it on just for noise in their too-quiet apartment. And of course it seemed like every show, every commercial, had cowboys in it, so she'd flip the station. About the only thing that didn't have cowboys were the numerous football games, so that was what played in the background while she'd prepared for the board meeting over the weekend.

Although she did draw the line and turned the TV off when the Dallas Cowboys game started. She was mad at the entire state of Texas for incarcerating Wyatt…and, well, the word *cowboys* was an arrow to her heart.

The mirrored doors of the elevator reflected back that yes, she did look as bad as she felt. Not even her top-of-the-line concealer could hide the smudges under her eyes. The pace at work was really taking its toll on top of sleepless nights spent aching for Wyatt. Once they got through the board meeting today, when, hopefully, the merger would be finalized, she could take a break. Maybe she and Johnny could go somewhere, relax. Maybe Hawaii. Get some sun on her pale cheeks.

The elevator stopped and she walked out into the lobby, then followed the same path she'd taken to her office the last nine years.

She walked into her corner office and dumped her purse and briefcase on the credenza, wanted to collapse into her chair. Monday morning and there was already a big stack of mail on her desk. Well, it would have to wait till after the board meeting.

Isabella walked into her office, handed her a cup of steaming black coffee. Not even seven thirty, yet her assistant always beat her in.

Francine sipped the coffee and winced. Not at all like Wyatt's coffee.

"Thanks. Have a good weekend?" she asked, not really listening to the standard answer her assistant always gave.

"Let me say first that I am so sorry, Ms. Wentworth," Isabella said.

This was new. "What's wrong?" Isabella had been with her all these years, and she'd never looked so upset.

"I forgot to give this to you on Friday night. Again, I'm so sorry," Isabella said, holding out a bulky white envelope with the company logo embossed on it. "It got buried in a pile of papers on my desk, and I just found it."

Francine took the envelope and started to open it, saw Isabella leaving and shutting her door, which was very odd.

She pulled out a single piece of paper, and a long thin box fell out onto the desk.

Frankie, I'm here in New York. I love you.
   Forgive me for pushing you away.
   I'll be waiting for you in the coffee shop downstairs.
Love, Wyatt.
PS Housekeeping found your necklace.

Her hands trembled so much she dropped the note on top of the box.

Isabella had said she forgot to give it to Francine Friday night. He'd been here? In the lobby? And she wasn't told?

She pushed the buzzer on the intercom, and the door opened almost immediately.

Isabella walked in like she was heading to the guillotine. "I'll understand if you fire me."

"I'm not going to fire you. But why didn't you get me out of the meeting?"

"Whatever that cowboy had to say couldn't have been more important than the meeting you were in. I know everything hinges on the board meeting today. Your father would have been livid and fired me, or worse, if I'd pulled you out."

"That'll be all," Francine said, hating the wobble in her voice. "Shut the door, please."

The door closed quietly behind Isabella, and Francine dropped into her chair. She picked the note up, traced her finger over every word, every letter.

She felt like a teenager holding her boyfriend's note, knowing he'd written it just for her.

God, she missed him. He'd opened up so much since the first time she met him. Was it just a month ago? She missed his voice, his laugh, the way his full lips quirked when he teased her about something.

She missed the gentle way he had with her son. That he never talked down to Johnny. His fierce protectiveness for both of them.

She missed the way he held her tight, and the way she always felt safe with him. Her eyes started watering, and she lost the battle not to cry.

The door opened. "Are you ready for—" Her father stopped short. "What is it? What's wrong?"

He'd never understand, but she had to try.

"I just found out Wyatt came to see me on Friday, but no one told me," she said, grabbing a tissue and wiping her tears.

"What the hell was he doing here?"

"He came to tell me—"

"Never mind. It doesn't matter. I'll deal with it later," he said. "Do you have your notes ready? I want us in the boardroom, a united front, when the board walks in."

He opened the door, but she stayed in her chair.

"It doesn't matter?" she repeated. "Of course it matters."

"Francine, nothing matters except getting this merger finalized with the board members today." He came back in and leaned on her desk. "You know damn good and well what's at stake here."

She touched the note from Wyatt again, like a talisman. "Yeah, I do. Love."

Her dad pushed off the desk. "Screw that. This is important to me, to us. To my damn company."

"Is money all you care about?"

"I haven't seen you complain about having it. What, you want to chuck it all and go live in the middle of nowhere with that ranch hand? He's not right for you. He even admitted it to me himself."

She rose, barely keeping her tone civil. "He's a hell of a lot more than a ranch hand. He has standards, morals, values. He cares about his family, the land. He cares about me and Johnny. And I think he's perfect for us."

"Stop with that ridiculous nickname."

"Do you know why Wyatt calls him Johnny? He lets him be a kid, not a little version of *you*. Johnny was happy on the ranch. When was the last time you saw him laugh before we left for Montana?"

Her father looked taken aback as he paced away, then back to her desk. "You're an important part of my company. I was going to announce it after the board meeting, but I'll tell you now. I'm promoting you to chief operating officer, effective immediately."

The news left her reeling. She'd worked hard all her life to get here. Now she was a step closer to CEO. "Wow. I can't believe it. I—" She glanced at the note on her desk, and the seed of a doubt unfurled in her stomach. "When did you decide to promote me? Before or after you found out about this?" She waved the note in the air.

"Doesn't matter. I'm still promoting you. What you've always wanted. We'll be running my company—our company—together."

The picture in the ornate glass frame on her desk caught her eye. Johnny.

Being COO would mean even more hours. Less time with her sweet baby boy.

She remembered all those times she'd sat in her father's office late at night as he worked. Hoping for his attention, that he'd spend time with her outside the office.

"Why aren't you happy about the promotion?" he asked.

She looked up at him. "Do you know why I started working here?" She spoke slowly. "I don't love this job or this company. I just wanted you to love me..."

"I've always loved you. But after the divorce, and your mother leaving to find herself, I didn't know how to be a dad. All I knew was work." He faltered, checking his watch. "Let's talk later tonight, okay? Right now we need to get to the boardroom." He kissed her cheek and walked out the door.

This was a dream come true. She'd hoped of becoming CEO one day after her father retired, and now, the opportunity to actually have a say in running the company was happening much faster than she'd thought.

But at what cost?

Chapter Twenty-Three

Wyatt drove the tractor into the barn, shut the engine down and climbed off. Nash sat on the stool by the workbench.

"I'm sorry things didn't work out for you in New York."

Wyatt shrugged.

"Wanna talk about it?"

"Nope."

"You've been calm since you got back—too calm."

He finally looked up at his oldest brother. "And that's a problem?"

"It is when there's stuff building up inside. You need a way to let it go."

"So I should go back to throwing things around? Punching holes in walls?"

"Didn't say that." Nash pulled a card out of his pocket. "This is someone my counselor recommended."

Wyatt stared at the little white card but didn't touch it. "I don't need to talk to a shrink."

"He's not a shrink, he's a grief counselor. I think if you talk to someone, get those feelings out in the open—"

"That's just it. I don't feel anything."

And he hadn't since he realized a few days ago—a lifetime ago—that Frankie and Johnny would never be his. Seeing her in furs and jewels, something he could never give her, hit home the point—they were too different. Now he was completely numb.

"That's not good, either." Nash stood up. "If you won't go see a counselor, you can always talk to one of us. We're here for you, bro."

Nash walked to the door, the permanent limp a reminder of what he'd suffered and lost.

A little crack opened in Wyatt's heart at his brother's concern, and he pushed the heel of his hand against his chest. "Nash, thanks. I mean it."

"That's what family's for. Come have dinner with us tonight. You can let Maddy trounce you at Candy Land."

Wyatt's mouth kicked up in half a grin, but as soon as Nash left, it slid off his face.

The last thing he needed was to be around a family like Nash's tonight. It would remind him too much of what he'd lost.

He spent the rest of the day repairing some of the multitude of things on his never-ending list. Sure, he could delegate, but he liked fixing things. He'd always been good with his hands.

Now it just kept him busy till he could fall into bed at night and not think.

His stomach growled, reminding him he hadn't eaten since who knew when. He took a few minutes to clean up the workbench and decided to see what Mrs. Green could whip up for him at the lodge for dinner. He'd make his excuses to Nash in the morning.

Following the path to the lodge, he thought he heard laughter. He paused, heard it again. It sounded like it was coming from the mud pit—or rather, the still-not-planted vegetable garden. Mrs. Green had been bugging him about it every chance she could. Too late for planting now, it'd be ready for spring.

"Damn kids," he muttered. Probably the triples and Toby messing around. They couldn't resist a muddy hole. Pretty much like him and his brothers when they were growing up.

He stepped off the sidewalk and cut across the grass, remembering that the last time he'd walked this way had been the day he'd met Frankie.

He almost tripped over a garden hose snaking across the grass, and he looked up to see who was playing with it.

Frankie.

In the mud pit.

He shook his head, squeezed his eyes shut tight.

Opened them again.

Not a mirage.

Frankie was in the mud pit, hosing down the whole area, wearing a cream-colored coat, copper-colored slacks and high heels. Johnny squatted at the side of the pit, laughing.

"Frankie?" he croaked, still not believing it.

She looked up at him and dropped the hose, then crooked her finger and beckoned him closer.

"What're you doing?" He wanted to run to her and Johnny, but his damn feet wouldn't move, and he was frozen in place.

"Having fun." She plopped down into the mud, then lay down and moved her arms and legs.

Suddenly his feet unstuck and he walked closer.

She was making a snow angel—in the mud.

Johnny was rolling on the ground, laughing, his giggles the best sound Wyatt had heard in a long time. "Mr. Wyatt!" He got up and launched himself at Wyatt.

"Hey, bud. I missed you so much," he said, swinging Johnny up into a hug. "I don't get it," he said to her, standing at the edge of the pit.

She finally stopped moving and sat up, held her hand out to him. "Help me up and I'll explain."

He set Johnny down and leaned forward, grabbed her hand. But she put her other hand on his and yanked, pulling him down on top of her in the mud.

She grabbed a handful of mud and smeared it on his cheek. Then wrapped her legs around his and rolled him over so he was flat on his back.

Mud oozed all around him, the cold seeping through his flannel shirt. But he didn't care, not if it meant she was back.

She sat up, still on his thighs. She huffed and fisted her hands on her hips. "Well? Aren't you going to say anything?"

"I don't understand. Why are you here? You must hate me."

"I don't hate you. You came to New York."

"I waited seven hours for you. When you finally came out of the office, you never even looked my way."

Her face softened, and her hands dropped from her hips. "I'm so sorry. I didn't know you were at my office. My assistant forgot to give me the envelope until this morning."

"How'd you get here so fast if you just got my note this morning?"

"I swiped the keys to Daddy's jet."

He laughed, then saw she wasn't smiling. "You serious?"

"Yup. Well, metaphorical keys. I called the pilot and had him gas up the company jet, file a flight plan. The board meeting finished early—merger complete—so I ran home, packed a few things and Johnny and I sped to the airport."

"Did you talk to your dad?"

"I told him I don't want Johnny to grow up only getting to spend time with me in the office, like I did with my own father. I thanked him for the promotion to COO—"

He held a hand up. "Wait a minute. He gave you a promotion to that level? And you turned it down? I thought that's what you've always wanted."

Frankie was shaking her head even before he finished speaking. "I realized I don't want to have a prestigious title and no family life. I want love. I want you. It's so beautiful out here, and Johnny loves it. He's never been truly happy in New York, but it took our trip out here for me to realize *neither* of us were happy there."

She cupped his cheeks, and he pressed a kiss to her freezing-cold palm. "You're what I want, Wyatt. I love you so much." She kissed him, and he thought his brain would ooze out his ears. "So what was your question?"

"What question?"

"You know, from the note you left me."

It took a few seconds for her words to register through the fog in his brain.

"I was going to ask you to marry me."

"You *were* going to ask me—past tense. And now?"

"Will you marry me? Will you and Johnny be my family?"

"You better believe it, cowboy."

And she kissed him again. Her lips were freezing, his ass was freezing in the mud and it felt like mud was in every pore of his body.

But he didn't care. He wrapped her in his arms, held her so tight she'd never get free.

"Yay!" Johnny shouted, jumping up and down.

She broke the kiss and sat up, reached over and picked Johnny up, set him down in the mud pit.

Wyatt looked at Frankie, then at Johnny, and grabbed

handfuls of mud at the same time she did, and they both smeared it on Johnny's coat and khaki pants.

"So now I can be a real live cowboy?" Johnny asked.

"Yup," Wyatt said, and pulled Johnny and Frankie into a very muddy hug.

Frankie laughed, tears streaking down her beautiful mud-covered face. "You know what they say—the family that plays in the mud together, stays together."

And just like that, gone was the pain, gone was his past, gone was the feeling of being alone forever. Sitting in the dirt, he felt washed clean, ready to start a new life.

Epilogue

One week later, and it was her wedding day. Kelsey and Bunny had thrown themselves into a flurry of activity with plans. And Francine was extremely grateful for their help. If it had been up to her, she, Wyatt and Johnny would have headed to the courthouse to be married.

But Bunny had pooh-poohed that idea and told her weddings were an important start to any marriage.

Francine had already had a big society wedding the first time around—for a marriage that had ended disastrously. This time, she was more than happy to have a quiet wedding with just family and a few friends, right here on the ranch.

The one thing that put a dark spot on what should have been her happiest day ever was her father. She'd tried calling, sent him an email—and an invitation—asking him to come to her wedding. She'd even copied his assistant to make sure he read the email and opened the invitation.

He hadn't responded.

Obviously he wasn't happy she'd left the company. Or that she was marrying Wyatt. But couldn't he at least have flown out to walk her down the aisle?

Bunny came to the rescue, however, and volunteered Angus to stand in for her father.

Now it was almost time for Angus to meet her and begin

the processional. At least she had some family there—Johnny had been excited to be the ring bearer.

And Maddy had been so adorable about asking if she could be the flower girl. Francine loved the idea as much as she'd come to love Maddy. That sweet little girl, at only six years of age, had taken Johnny under her wing and made sure he became a solid part of the Sullivan cousins. They were all inseparable, except when Hunter's boys had to go back and live with their mother in town.

Bunny handed her a glass of champagne. "Let's have one more check of your dress, shall we?"

Francine faced the mirror in the bridal suite of the lodge. She'd wanted a simple dress and found one in ivory with a sweetheart neckline, short sleeves, a lace overlay to the fitted bodice, and a tulle skirt. Simple, understated, elegant.

She pulled the skirt up enough to let her ivory cowboy boots peek out. Wyatt had found them for her, and she loved them. Forgoing a veil, she'd just curled her hair and pulled it back on one side with a silver comb.

A knock sounded at the door. Bunny opened it a crack, then let Kelsey in.

"Oh, Frankie. You look beautiful!" Kelsey sniffled into a handkerchief. "Damn pregnancy hormones."

"You feeling all right?" Francine asked her.

"Fine. I'm so happy for you and Wyatt."

Since they had bonded from the beginning of the working retreat, she'd asked Kelsey to be her matron of honor.

"I'm supposed to give this to you now, Frankie," Kelsey said and handed her a small white shopping bag.

Francine read the note on the bag.

In case you need something blue. Wyatt.

She opened the bag and pulled out a lacy white garter, then heard what sounded like a small bell. She turned the garter over and saw a miniature turquoise cowbell with writing on it.

I'll love you till the cows come home.

She burst out laughing and clutched it to her chest. For being such a brooding, enigmatic cowboy, Wyatt could always make her laugh. Raising her skirt, she immediately slipped it on over her boot and up her leg to sit just below her knee.

"Frankie, do you have your phone or a camera handy?" Bunny asked from beside the window.

She picked up her phone, held it up. "Why?"

"You've got to see this. It's the most adorable thing."

Francine walked to the window and peered out between the curtains. Wyatt and Johnny were walking up the path, dressed in matching outfits of dark jeans, white shirts, black ties, black vests and black tux jackets. And of course their matching black cowboy hats and boots.

Wyatt held Johnny's hand as they walked, deep in conversation, looking at each other.

Francine's eyes welled up, and she fumbled for the camera app, taking a ton of pictures through the window.

"You have to stop crying now, Frankie. You'll ruin your beautiful makeup," Kelsey said and handed her a tissue. "And then I'll have to start crying with you."

Another knock sounded at the door.

"That should be Angus to take you downstairs," Bunny said, and cracked the door open. "Oh, well. Hello," she said and stepped back.

The door opened wider, and Francine's father walked into the suite.

Bunny and Kelsey exchanged a glance then slipped out and quietly closed the door.

"Dad!"

"Am I still invited?"

She launched herself into his open arms. "Of course you are," she said, laughing and crying at the same time.

He hugged her tight, then stepped back, held her at arm's length. "You're a beautiful bride, Francine. You're glowing. I'm willing to admit I was wrong about Wyatt if he makes you this happy. I'm sorry, daughter."

"He does make me happy, and he loves Johnny like he was his own flesh and blood."

"That's good. Because if he ever makes you cry, or hurts you in any way, he'll have to answer to me."

"I didn't think you were coming."

"I almost didn't. I have to admit I was furious at you for leaving. But then I remembered what you said the day of the board meeting."

She cocked her head.

"You said you started working with me so I would notice you and love you. It broke my heart to have you think I don't truly love you. I've always been immensely proud of you, Francine. I don't want you to leave the company."

"Dad, I don't want to live in New York—none of us do. Wyatt and Johnny would both wither and die in that big city. And after falling in love with this place, I probably would, too."

Her father held a hand up. "That's not what I meant. What if you stay on as a consultant? You can work from here, fly in every so often if you're needed."

Francine grinned. "I think I'd like that. Can I talk to Wyatt later? I'm about to be a little busy for the next few hours."

"Of course. Take your time and let me know." He checked his watch. "Now, I think it's time we get you down the aisle, don't you?"

He opened the door to the suite, and she picked up her bouquet of sweetheart roses and linked her arm in his, so grateful he'd had a change of heart and come to see her get married.

And admit he was wrong about her soon-to-be husband.

WYATT HAD NEVER thought he'd settle down, much less get his own happy ending. But here he was, married and at their wedding reception.

Frankie looked so beautiful and radiant it had made his throat hurt, and he'd had to swallow back tears when she'd walked down the aisle.

It had been a shock to see her walking with her dad. No wonder she looked so happy. He figured that meant they'd made amends. The perfect gift for her, today of all days.

When the minister had pronounced them husband and wife, Johnny had run up to them and thrown his arms around Wyatt. "Now can I call you Daddy?" he'd blurted loud enough for everyone to hear.

The reception in full swing, Wyatt looked around at everyone having a good time. He gazed at Frankie as she laughed with Isabella, the dragon assistant who had flown out for the wedding. Isabella had apologized to him for forgetting to give Frankie the envelope that night. He'd said it was over and done, and at least they were together now.

Johnny ran up to him, another s'mores cupcake in his hand. He and Frankie had decided to surprise Johnny with his favorite dessert, and the kid had been so excited he'd dropped the first one.

"How many of those have you had, bud?" Wyatt asked, grabbing a napkin and wiping Johnny's mouth.

"I dunno, Daddy," Johnny mumbled around a mouthful.

"You might want to slow down. I promise we'll have some left over." He crouched down to Johnny's level. "And I betcha Mrs. Green would make more if we do run out."

Johnny grinned, then smacked Wyatt's cheek with a kiss and ran off to find Maddy.

He stood up just as Frankie walked up to him and started to kiss him, then pulled back. She picked up a napkin and wiped his cheek. "Chocolate. Johnny?" She laughed.

"Yup. I hope he doesn't have a stomachache later. That would ruin the sleepover with the cousins."

"Not to mention our wedding night," Frankie whispered in his ear.

Her lips tickled his ear, and it was all he could do not to snatch her away right now and start their wedding night early. They'd hardly had any time alone since the week before when she and Johnny arrived.

And now that she truly was his wife, he wanted her with a passion he'd never experienced until now. When they'd had their first dance a short time ago, he'd ached for her. She'd brushed against him, then smiled that siren smile she saved only for him. And she'd whispered in his ear what she wanted to do as soon as they reached his— their—cabin.

Before he could try to convince her to sneak out, Frankie got pulled away to talk to someone else.

And he mentally ticked down the seconds till they could leave.

"Hey, bro," Hunter said and swung an arm around Wyatt's neck. "You are one lucky dude to have such a good-lookin' bride."

"You ready to settle down again?" Wyatt asked him.

"Hell, no. I'm having too much fun being single."

Wyatt looked at his youngest brother—there was something odd in his tone. "You sure about that?"

Hunter grinned, toasted Wyatt with his beer bottle. "You bet. Footloose and fancy-free. So I'm going to go talk to that woman from Frankie's office." He peeled off and walked toward Isabella.

Wyatt looked around and found Frankie. "Can we go yet? I want to take you home and make you mine for good," he whispered in her ear.

She smiled, then leaned in and brushed a kiss across his mouth. "Yes. Bunny just told me it's time to throw the bouquet so we can leave."

The DJ's call for all the single women to gather around the dance floor had them squealing and rushing forward. Even Isabella looked excited about joining in. She and Hunter had just started talking, but she edged away toward the group of singles.

And just like that, Wyatt flashed back to Nash's wedding a couple months ago. Wyatt had been talking to a woman as Kelsey threw her bouquet. It had hit him in the head, and he'd reflexively caught the flowers.

When he realized what had happened, he'd tried to get Kelsey to rethrow it, but she refused.

And now he was married.

He grinned, watching Frankie prepare to throw her own bouquet.

It had worked out just fine, him catching that fated bouquet. No complaints from his corner. Nope. None at all.

"Three, two, one!" Frankie hollered and tossed it over her head.

He watched the flowers sailing through the air almost as if they were in slow motion, turquoise ribbons trailing like a kite tail.

Hunter turned around, holding a piece of paper out toward Isabella, and the flowers landed in his outstretched hand.

Wyatt started laughing as Hunter stared at them, a look of horror on his face.

"Frankie!" Hunter yelled. "Do it over!"

She linked her arm with Wyatt's. "No way, brother. You're next!" she called.

Wyatt couldn't stop laughing, and tears gathered in his eyes. He wiped them away with his thumb.

"What's so funny?" Frankie asked.

"Fate, Frankie. Fate."

He'd gone from a rebellious cowboy to a groom, all because of a bouquet of flowers that hit him in the head, and the pit of mud Frankie had fallen in that first day.

In that moment, as he took her hand to walk out of the reception, he knew, without a doubt, he'd never been happier in his life.

* * * * *

If you loved this book, look for the previous book in Allison B. Collins's COWBOYS TO GROOMS *series:*

A FAMILY FOR THE RANCHER

Available now at Harlequin.com!

We hope you enjoyed this story from
Harlequin® Western Romance.

Harlequin® Western Romance is coming to an end, but community, cowboys and true love are here to stay. Starting July 2018, discover more heartfelt tales of family and friendship from **Harlequin® Special Edition**.

Romance is for life, and these stories show that every chapter in a relationship has its challenges and delights and that love can be renewed with each turn of the page!

Look for six *new* romances every month from **Harlequin® Special Edition!**
Available wherever books are sold.

HWRST0318

SPECIAL EXCERPT FROM

HARLEQUIN®

SPECIAL EDITION

*Days before her thirtieth birthday, Allegra Clark finds
herself a runaway bride and accidentally crashing a
birthday party for Zander Wilde—the man who promised
to marry her if neither of them was married by thirty…*

*Read on for a sneak preview of
HOW TO ROMANCE A RUNAWAY BRIDE,
the next book in the **WILDE HEARTS** miniseries,
by Teri Wilson.*

Is that what you want? The question was still there, in his
eyes. All she had to do was decide.

She took a deep breath and shook her head.

Zander leaned closer, his eyes hard on hers. Then he
reached to cup her face with his free hand and drew the
pad of his thumb slowly, deliberately along the swell of
her bottom lip. "Tell me what you want, Allegra."

You. She swallowed. *I want you.*

"This," she said, reaching up on tiptoe to close the
space between them and touch her lips to his.

What are you doing? Stop.

But it was too late to change her mind. Too late to
pretend she didn't want this. Because the moment her
mouth grazed Zander's, he took ownership of the kiss.

His hands slid into her hair, holding her in place, while
his tongue slid brazenly along the seam of her lips until
they parted, opening for him.

Then there was nothing but heat and want and the
shocking reality that this was what she'd wanted all
along. Zander.

Had she always felt this way? It seemed impossible. Yet beneath the newness of his mouth on hers and the crush of her breasts against the solid wall of his chest, there was something else. A feeling she couldn't quite put her finger on. A sense of belonging. Of destiny.

Home.

Allegra squeezed her eyes closed. She didn't want to imagine herself fitting into this life again. There was too much at stake. Too much to lose. But no matter how hard she railed against it, there it was, shimmering before like her a mirage.

She whimpered into Zander's mouth, and he groaned in return, gently guiding her backward until her spine was pressed against the cool marble wall. Before she could register what was happening, he gathered her wrists and pinned them above her head with a single, capable hand. And the last remaining traces of resistance melted away. She couldn't fight it anymore. Not from this position of delicious surrender. Her arms went lax, and somewhere in the back of her mind, a wall came tumbling down.

The breath rushed from her body, and a memory came into focus with perfect, crystalline clarity.

Let's make a deal. If neither of us is married by the time we turn thirty, we'll marry each other. Agreed?

Agreed?

HARLEQUIN

Western Romance

Romance—the Western way!

Cathy Gillen Thacker

introduces a new family of sexy and stubborn
cowboys in *Texas Legends: The McCabes* series

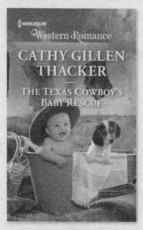

Texas Legends: The McCabes

The Texas Cowboy's Baby Rescue (April 2018)

The Texas Cowboy's Triplets (June 2018)

Don't miss the next installment,
THE TEXAS COWBOY'S QUADRUPLETS,
coming to Harlequin Special Edition October 2018.

SPECIAL EDITION

HWRCGT0618R

Reward the book lover in you!

Earn points from all your Harlequin book purchases from wherever you shop.

Turn your points into *FREE BOOKS* of your choice
OR
EXCLUSIVE GIFTS from your favorite authors or series.

Join for FREE today at
www.HarlequinMyRewards.com.

Harlequin My Rewards is a free program (no fees) without any commitments or obligations.

MYR17